Triple Play

RHYANNON BYRD

ELLORA'S CAVE
ROMANTICA PUBLISHING

An Ellora's Cave Romantica Publication

www.ellorascave.com

Triple Play

ISBN 1419953060, 9781419953064
ALL RIGHTS RESERVED.
Triple Play Copyright © 2005 Rhyannon Byrd
Edited by Pamela Campbell.
Cover art by Syneca.

This book printed in the U.S.A. by Jasmine–Jade Enterprises, LLC.

Electronic book Publication June 2005
Trade paperback Publication December 2005

Also by Rhyannon Byrd

ഔ

About the Author

૪૭

Rhyannon Byrd is the wife of a Brit, mother of two amazing children, and maid to a precocious beagle named Misha. A longtime fan of romance, she finally felt at home when she read her first Romantica® novel. Her love of this spicy, ever-changing genre has become an unquenchable passion—the hotter they are, the better she enjoys them!

Writing for Ellora's Cave is a dream come true for Rhyannon. Now her days (and let's face it, most nights) are spent giving life to the stories and characters running wild in her head. Whether she's writing contemporaries, paranormals…or even futuristics, there's always sure to be a strong Alpha hero featured as well as a fascinating woman to capture his heart, keeping all that wicked wildness for her own!

Rhyannon welcomes comments from readers. You can find her website and email address on her author bio page at www.ellorascave.com.

Tell Us What You Think

We appreciate hearing reader opinions about our books. You can email us at Comments@EllorasCave.com.

TRIPLE PLAY

⚮

To my readers:

I created the *Sexy Sweet* series as my Romantica® playground—a place where I could try my hand at/experiment with different genres and themes to see what types of deeply emotional, scorching tales I could create for you, my readers. *Triple Play* is the first book in the series, and offers a provocative glimpse into the ménage a trois, one of erotic romance's most scintillating genres. Future stories will look into the compelling worlds of exhibitionism and BDSM, as well as shapeshifters, paranormals, and interracial romance. As you can see, it's going to be one long, wicked ride, and I invite you to join me for the fun as we venture into the multi-faceted, always fascinating realm of human sexuality.

For this first book, it's my hope that you will lose yourself in this erotically seductive interlude as it carries us through a breathtaking evening spent with three characters exploring the vivid world of ménage. With raw emotion and primal passions, they embark upon a road of carnal discovery in the hope that it will lead them not only to ultimate pleasure, but to that all too wonderful happily-ever-after and undeniable love that we simply cannot live without.

The next two interludes are already planned: exhibitionism and BDSM. One of which is the suitably sizzling story of a certain mischievous, "sexy as all get out" redhead featured in this tale.

Many thanks,
Rhyannon Byrd

Dedication

There are so many people for me to thank, but being that this is my first dedication, I must start with my sexy Brit, who makes everything possible. Thank you for being so beautifully supportive and such a wonderful husband and friend; for listening to me complain endlessly when I can't get a story "just" right; and for always pushing me to do my absolute best and follow my dreams.

You're amazing, sweetheart, and I love you!

Trademarks Acknowledgement

&

The author acknowledges the trademarked status and trademark owners of the following word marks mentioned in this work of fiction:

Cristal Champagne: Champagne Louis Roederer

Audi: Audi A.G. Corporation

Chivas: Chivas Brothers (Americas) Limited

Giorgio Armani: GA Modefine S.A. Corporation

Mack: Mack Trucks, Inc.

Porsche: Dr. Ing. h.c. F. Porsche

Chapter One

🔊

Who would have ever thought that a girl could lose her heart in a hallway?

It was kind of pathetic—but unfortunately, for Denny Abbott, it was entirely true.

"Get a grip, girl," Denny muttered to herself, clutching her armful of file folders and a single cardboard-tasting diet bar tighter against her chest, her heart hammering like a bass drum, unable to rip her eyes away from the ruggedly handsome sight he made. The floor could have opened up at her feet, her next step plunging her to a painful, bone-shattering death, and she wouldn't have known, because she couldn't look away from him.

"It's never gonna happen—even in your wildest dreams," she whispered, knowing that those gray eyes were watching her, fearing that her feelings were written all over her flushed face for him to see in all their embarrassing glory.

He walked down the sunlit corridor toward her, the same way he had the day she'd been on her way to her first interview with him, and the second she'd set eyes on him—meltdown. Total, complete, undeniable emotional and sexual meltdown, and it was happening again.

The noonday sun burned like a ball of fire in the distant sky that lay beyond the far wall of glass, glowing around his broad, sleekly muscled physique, as if he were an ancient god come down from Olympus. He was all hard, dominant lines and raw-edged power—long, strong bones and powerful, starkly defined musculature, moving with the arrogant strength of a lethal predator.

Damn, just the sight of him made her mouth water, her heart ache. "You're an idiot, Denny. He's God's gift to womankind, and you're...you're like the chubby little girl eyeing those forbidden sweets through the candy store window. Do your pride a favor and get hold of yourself."

Yeah, it was good advice, only...the only thing she wanted to get hold of was Gabriel Harrison.

And it didn't help that he looked good enough to eat. It wasn't even that he was the most handsome man she'd ever seen, though handsome he was. No, it was the power and masculine grace with which he held himself, the Armani suit doing little to hide the devastatingly male animal that lurked beneath. The expensive clothes were nothing but a thin veneer of wealth and civilization that Denny saw right through. Saw straight past, right down to the carnal cravings and primal appetites that lived within, beneath all those deadening layers of emotional ice and calculated control.

Everything about him pulled her in, from the harsh air of loneliness, to the dangerous looking scars. Ah...and there was the real kicker. She'd been suckered in by her soft, feminine soul, duped into believing she could be the "one" woman who could heal whatever past hurts he carried on his broad shoulders like a cloak of penance. She wanted him to open his heart and invite her all the way inside. Wanted to crawl inside of him through the wicked beauty of that scarred mouth until she found the icy chill of his heart and warmed it within her palms, pulling it into the giving heat of her chest, nestled between her breasts, until it beat in time with her own.

He enthralled her, all that inner physical strength that he kept under such tight control, those dark brooding looks and cold gray eyes that she wanted to melt with sunshine and smiles. Wanted to bask in the breathtaking beauty of a warm, genuine smile breaking across that wickedly sinful mouth, crinkling the dark corners of that piercing metallic gaze.

She wanted to warm his soul, to give him everything she had, was, and could ever be—if he'd only let her love him.

Every step she took down the long length of the corridor brought them closer together, and just like that first day, Denny wanted to rip off her clothes and throw herself at his feet, begging him to devour her on the ravaging altar of his lust.

"Oh God, I've been reading too many gothic romance novels," she moaned beneath her breath. *Ravaging altar of his lust!* A hysterical giggle choked in the back of her throat at the ridiculous thought, but damn if it wasn't true. As campy as it sounded, she'd jump at the chance to sacrifice herself at the hands of Gabriel Harrison.

There were just two rather strong points working against her. Well three, if she was perfectly honest with herself. One, he was her boss. Two, he was lethally sexy and could have any woman he wanted. And three, she was Denise "Denny" Abbott.

Just plain, plump Denny, with long brown hair and big brown eyes, wrapped up in sale-rack clothing, like the lowly serf staring with starry eyes up at the castle window of the arrogant prince.

Only, Gabriel Harrison wasn't an arrogant snob. Far from it. He worked his ass off for the company he owned with four of his friends. Worked with the inhuman skill of a cyborg, as if the normal restrictions of mankind didn't apply to him. She'd have thought he was a machine, if it weren't for the scars—but there was no way to mistake them for anything other than savage signs of his mortality.

No more than ten feet separated them now, and she could barely breathe. It was ridiculous. She'd worked with him for months now, seen him nearly every day, and still she couldn't control herself—knew she had be blasting "I'm desperate and I want you!" like a neon sign across her forehead, proclaiming her obsession for the entire world to see.

"Damn, Denny, you need to get laid, girl," she quietly grumbled, trying to prepare herself to say hello without drooling, when WHAM!, the office door in front of her opened and she ran smack into Diana Colby.

"Yikes!" she cried, and her armful of possessions went scattering across the hallway, papers flying out of their folders to flitter in the air, caught in the brilliant splash of sunlight as it streamed in through the far glass wall. "Oh my God, I'm so sorry," she rambled, wishing she could just sink into the floor as she knelt down and started collecting her scattered sheaves of paper.

Diana made no move to help her, but Denny really didn't care. The sooner the snide woman left, the better. Diana worked in the human resources department, and it seemed that she always went out of her way to make other women feel miserable, which made no sense to Denny. It wasn't like she was any competition for the tall, elegantly slim, blonde executive.

"Oh Denny, I'm sorry," Diana drawled, looking down at her with a smug smile clearly indicating she was anything but. "I didn't see you there. Hard to believe I could miss you, though, isn't it?" Her smile widened, and then she turned toward Gabriel, who now stood at their side. To Denny's horror, she realized the diet bar she'd been planning on choking down for her lunch lay right beside his Italian loafer-covered left foot, and quickly snatched it up.

"Gabriel," Diana all but purred. "You're looking as edible as ever."

"*Mrs.* Colby," he replied, putting an extra emphasis on the "Mrs." that Denny knew the other woman couldn't miss, before bending down to helpfully pick up the last handful of papers and hand them to her. She sent him a wan smile, noting that his gray eyes glittered with some unknown expression, and watched with held breath as he moved back to his full height.

"Thanks," she finally whispered, hating how she felt kneeling at the blonde goddess' feet, like a frumpy maid bowing before the lady of the manor. *Get a backbone, you ninny!*

Diana smiled a cool smile at Gabriel, then turned an angry, narrow-eyed look down at Denny that had her blinking in confusion at what looked suspiciously like jealousy. *Sheesh*, she thought, *some women were so odd*.

"Try to keep your eyes off your feet and watch where you're going, Denny," Diana delivered with such false sweetness, it made Denny want to snort. "Really, you never know what kind of accidents your clumsiness may cause."

Ouch! Denny gasped, feeling her face flush as the woman turned on her spiked heel and strolled away, her slim hips moving in a seductive rhythm that had probably snagged the attention of the man standing beside her like a bear to honey.

"And maybe you should try being less of a vicious bitch," she softly muttered, stuffing the loose papers she'd planned on working on during lunch back into their folders.

"I heard that," came the deep, dark voice from up above, and she felt her stomach sink into her bent knees. Damn. He must have been watching her after all, instead of ogling ol' Diana. No way could her whisper have caught his attention otherwise. With as much dignity as she could claw onto, Denny rose to her feet and tried to smile, even though her face felt brittle. "Um...sorry about that."

His eyes flashed with irritation, maybe even anger, and she steeled herself, only to realize with a warm rush of surprise that it wasn't directed at her. "You'll have no arguments from me. I'm just wondering why you didn't say it to her face?"

"Oh...uh, I'm not much into confrontation," she replied lamely, and she could have sworn she saw the corner of his scarred mouth twitch with humor.

"There's a hell of a difference between looking for a fight, and standing up for yourself when someone is being an ass. Don't let her walk all over you, Den—Miss Abbott."

Oh crap. It was happening again. She could feel the soft, dazed look of love falling helplessly over her flushed features, and watched his eyes widen just a fraction, flashing with hunger and heat, before going coldly empty once again. It was as if he could simply flip a switch inside his head to turn emotions off and on—or maybe she was just imagining the entire thing—all of it. The heat and the hunger. The cold emptiness. She honestly didn't know what to believe.

But she'd come to know enough about Gabriel Harrison to believe, with absolute conviction, that he wasn't the cold-hearted bastard he projected to the world. Though he shrouded himself in an air of brutal, chilled control, Denny could feel the roiling fires of heat...of passion that he kept buried deep within, hidden beneath that intimidating wall of ice. Yeah, she could feel it...*feel him*, whenever he was near, as if some dark, needy, hungry part of him was calling out to her.

She wanted to be the "one". The one he came to. The one he needed. The one to ease that hunger and those fleeting glimpses of pain that—if you looked closely enough beneath the dangerous good looks and intimidating scars—could be witnessed there, in his deep gray eyes.

There were even times when she'd catch him looking her way, and the intensity of those dark looks held the power to make her melt, her body going warm and soft like heated caramel, whether they were from the other side of a conference table or passing in the hall, like today. And sometimes...*oh, sometimes*...those big, hair-sprinkled hands would reveal the barest tremble, long fingers flexing, and then fiercely clenching. It was foolish, she knew, but Denny dreamed that at those times he struggled not to reach out for her, grab hold and take her with a desperation that demanded satisfaction.

God, I've got it so bad I'm becoming delusional, she muttered to herself. *Freaking certifiable.*

The sad fact was that Gabriel Harrison had never— *never*—said anything to suggest that he might actually be interested in her. Hell, this was the most he'd ever even spoken to her, when he wasn't working, dictating a proposal or changes to a contract.

They stood there, trapped in the strangely charged moment, neither of them moving, and then she noticed the muscle twitching in his hard jaw, that telltale tremble in his right hand before he shoved them both deep into the pockets of his slacks. "You..." he rasped, deep voice guttural and hoarse, "You're—"

Denny waited in heart-stopping expectation for him to finish his words, but he suddenly paused, as if catching himself, and then quickly growled, "Just put Diana Colby in her place next time."

"Yeah, I hear there's always room in hell," she joked with a small smile, trying to hide her disappointment, wondering what he'd been about to say, so eager to know what it was that she was damn near ready to grab his shoulders and shake it out of him. She was *what*, damn it? Beautiful? An idiot? The woman of his dreams? A first-class pain in the ass? Grrrr...anything would be better than not knowing what words had been hovering there on the tip of his tongue.

And then suddenly a small sigh caught in her throat, the understanding coming with a resigned acceptance of reality and fact. She couldn't force him to reveal himself to her, and she couldn't rage or curse him for not loving her in return. How could she? She knew he'd never done anything to encourage the impetuous emotion, one which ruled her heart with a mind of its own. No, the opposite was true. Gabriel Harrison, from the moment they'd first met, had done everything in the world to keep that cold, calculated distance between them—but her insensible heart hadn't cared.

Hell, it still didn't care.

The silence stretched out between them, and he swiftly broke their stare, dropping his gaze to the bundle of folders she held in her arms. "I don't expect you to work during your lunch hour, Miss Abbott."

She tried for a small smile, knowing it fell short. "Everyone else in my office was scheduled for that legal seminar I attended last month, so I just thought I'd catch up on some stuff."

He nodded, clearly not liking the idea, and then his gray gaze snagged on the diet bar she held in her right hand, clutched against the bulging file folders, and she silently groaned.

"What the hell is that?" he demanded, pulling one hand out of his pocket to grab the plastic-wrapped bar from her trembling fingers.

"Uh…that's just my lunch," she muttered, cheeks burning, feeling like an idiot. She knew she needed to lose weight, damn it, but it was embarrassing as hell having that fact flaunted in his face. Especially when he was so impossibly gorgeous.

Daaaamn. Where was a blasted hole in the floor when you needed one?

His gaze lowered, scanning the writing on the plastic wrapping, a scowl forming between the straight black lines of his brows as he caught her wide-eyed look. "Christ," he swore, those high cheekbones going dark with color. Despite her irritation and embarrassment, she watched in fascination as he worked his strong jaw, then grated out, "You do *not* need to go a damn diet, Den—Miss Abbott."

Argh. Could this get any worse? "Not to be rude, but it's really not any of your concern what I do, Mr. Harrison." Holding out her hand, she said, "My lunch, if you don't mind."

His gray gaze darkened with irritation. "I'm afraid I'm making it my concern. I don't want you wasting away to some scrawny little twig with no ass, and bones poking out beneath your skin."

Denny gave a feminine snort, completely shocked by his words. "I hardly think I'm in any danger of *that* happening. Now, can I please have my lunch back?"

"No," he grunted, deliberately pocketing the bar.

Denny blinked slowly, too stunned to be angry. "What?"

"I said no," he repeated with a sharp, hard edge to his voice that usually demanded someone follow his orders.

Her mouth thinned, lashes lowering as she tried to read him. "Uhh...you can't do that."

He arched one black brow. "Just who in the hell do you think is going to stop me?"

She opened her mouth—once, twice, feeling like a fish sucking at water. "Then what am I supposed to eat?"

He shoved his hands deeper into his pockets, broad shoulders accentuated by his aggressive stance. "Go down to the café and order a decent lunch and eat some real food. You do *not* need to change...*anything*, and I don't want to see those ridiculous things again. Do you understand me?"

"You may be my employer," Denny gasped, lost somewhere between a strange anger and a warm glow that felt oddly like she'd just been paid a wonderful compliment, "but you do not have the right to tell me what to eat...what to do. You don't own me, Mr. Harrison."

His stormy, glittering gray eyes narrowed to challenging slits. "I'm not particularly interested with what I own and what I don't."

"What about your own lunch?" she asked, suddenly wondering if she had the nerve to ask him to join her. Not that she wasn't irritated with his high-handed, bullying tactics, but she was finding it hard to work up a proper temper when she was so strangely flattered by what he'd done. Her last boyfriend had tried to force-feed the damn diet bars down her throat, so intent had he been on molding her into what he considered the "perfect" woman.

But tall, dark, drop-dead gorgeous Gabriel Harrison apparently preferred her just the way she was, and the knowledge sent a blistering wave of heat through her quivering limbs.

"I have to take a conference call in my office," he finally explained, in answer to her question. "Just have your meal put on my personal tab. I insist, since I've stolen yours."

"I can take care of myself." She forced her features into a calm expression, determined to hide her disappointment. "I don't need a man to see that I get fed."

"Don't need one, or don't want one?" he asked, and she could tell that he hadn't wanted to voice the question, but had not been able to stop himself.

Hmm...as Alice would say. *Curiouser and curiouser.*

"What interest is it of yours?" she replied, surprising herself with her boldness.

His mouth thinned, pulling the scar on his face tight, and he turned to walk away, before suddenly turning back and saying, "Don't *ever* underestimate a man's interest, Miss Abbott. You never know what you might get shocked by."

Denny forced her chin high, straightening her shoulders as she tilted her face to the side and allowed a slow smile to curl the corners of her mouth. "And I might not shock as easily as you think, Mr. Harrison."

His jaw worked, but he only nodded, then turned and walked away.

Gabriel Harrison neared the end of the hallway, and knew that Denny's eyes had followed him the entire way. He ground his back teeth, hands clenched in his pockets to stop that goddamn trembling, wanting to turn back to her, but knowing it would only lead to disaster. Knowing she could see right through him, down to all the dark, dirty little secrets he kept locked deep inside. Hell, she'd always been able to read him, and the thought aroused him as much as it worried him.

It'd been that way from the beginning, which is why she was the only female assistant he'd ever had who hadn't threatened to leave by the end of the first week. They usually took one look at him and decided they either liked his money or his body, and when they realized he was offering neither, that he wanted nothing more than their skills in the office, they either balked or ran.

But Denny had always known how to handle him. His outbursts and temper, or cold demeanor, never fazed her, as if she saw deeper. Saw the reasons—the truth—of why he struggled to keep his distance. Shit, if he were smart, he would have said no—given the job to the reed-thin redhead who would have lobbied for his attention but never tempted him, instead of the first woman who ever twisted his heart with the mere sound of her husky voice.

But he hadn't been able to resist.

He'd known, from that first moment, that he had to do whatever it took to keep her in his life, close by, where he could at least have the stolen opportunities, like today, to see her and talk to her—struggling like hell not to grab hold of her and fuck the consequences. And she'd proven herself more than capable at doing her job. Hell, she was a powerhouse in the workplace, and had quickly become an invaluable part of the company.

Gabriel turned back at the corner, just in time to see her walk away, and it was all he could do not to go after her, catch her up in his arms, and take her back to his office, where he could enact every single one of the raunchy, frenzied, mind-shattering sexual fantasies he'd lived off of since first setting eyes on her. Christ, it felt as if he'd wanted her forever, but no matter how he'd looked at it, there was no way to fuck her, to wrap himself up in that decadent promise of soul-scorching warmth that her soft, sweet smiles offered, without falling victim to the raging emotions that underlined the attraction.

No, damn it. He needed to get it through his thick skull once and for all. Denny Abbott was not, nor was she ever going to be, *his*.

He swallowed the bitter taste of reality and forced himself to turn and head to his office. He'd bury himself in work, work until he couldn't fucking see straight, and maybe…just maybe, he'd be able to forget, for even a moment, how badly he wanted to bury himself balls-deep inside of his sexy little assistant.

Chapter Two

❧

The deep, black magic voice at her back was nearly enough to make Denny melt in her padded leather computer chair. Mellow and low, with that little rasp to it—like the evocative sound of bodies rolling over a crinkling bed of crisp, golden leaves in the height of a wind-tossed fall—the voice played through her blood like a meandering vine. It wove a teasing wake of arousal in its path, the tendrils of sound curling around her senses, comforting and warm, while beneath those soothing emotions played the little devil of desire that no woman could help but feel.

Jonah Cartwright, business partner and best friend of Gabriel Harrison, just had that kind of heady effect on the opposite sex—and Denny was no exception. It'd been rumored over friendly luncheons between her and her close-knit group of coworkers that Jonah's voice alone could bring a woman to orgasm. And sitting there in her chair, cozy and comfortable in her corner cubicle of the office she shared with those same three friends, Denny realized it was almost true. Suppressing the shiver that trembled through her tingling limbs, she could only thank God that Jonah's deadly appeal, while intoxicating, wasn't quite the one to do "it" for her.

Not that it wasn't potent as hell—just not the one she'd been waiting to hear whisper something dark and wicked in her ear. No, that one remained as distant and brooding as ever. With a disgusted frown, she recalled their brief interchange in the hallway, one week ago today, when Mr. Harrison had confiscated her lunch.

She kept thinking back to it, working over it, but she still couldn't decide if his actions had come from some kind of actual interest in her, or some other unknown reason that she couldn't figure out. Maybe if she'd been able to look at it logically, she'd have an answer, but when it came to Gabriel Harrison, her logic flew right out the window.

He growled at her, and her heart tripped, as if he'd whispered sweet nothings in her ear. It was ridiculous. She had it so bad, she wanted to seek out a priest for a freaking exorcism.

All he had to do was look at her, and she lost herself in breathtaking images of naked limbs and clutching hands, the two of them battling for sexual dominance over a silk-covered bed, going at each other like animals. It was funny, because she'd always been the "lie on your back and try to think your way to an orgasm" kind of woman, but she knew there'd be no thinking with a man like him. None. He'd fry her brain.

And the weirdest part was that he'd had lunch in the downstairs café every day since then, making it a point to get a good look at what she was eating. Her friends thought it was a riot, teasing her about it until she'd blushed so hard she'd wondered if her cheeks would ever lose the bright flush of crimson. She'd have called him a controlling jerk for his attitude, if it hadn't made her feel so dang mushy inside. But there'd been no warmth to go with his interest, just those deep, dark looks, the emotional distance between them as cold and solid as ever.

Jonah, on the other hand, was all play. There was just something about him, something warm and wickedly inviting, that made women smile, and Denny could already feel the corners of her mouth curling into a playful, somewhat shy, grin.

"What was that?" she asked with a light, genuine laugh, looking over her shoulder at the sleekly muscled, broad-shouldered giant with dark auburn hair kept just long enough for a woman to lock her fingers into. And then there were those eyes—a mesmerizing deep blue—the color of sun-splashed skies framed by thick lashes such a deep, dark red they were nearly black.

It was almost seven and everyone else had already headed home, but she'd been working hard to complete the last-minute changes Mr. Harrison had e-mailed down to her at five, wanting to have the contract ready for his approval first thing in the a.m. Her hands remained alert, poised over her keyboard, though Jonah managed to capture her full attention the moment their gazes locked.

A slow, mischief-made smile curled across the firm line of his lips, the subtle musk of his scent teasing her nose with its purely masculine appeal. "I asked if you'd like to be a birthday present. How 'bout it, beautiful?"

A birthday present?

Twisting in her chair, hands smoothing over her skirt-covered, dimpled knees, Denny cocked her head to the side, wondering what the sexy hunk was up to. Aware of the dangers that came with flirting in the workplace, Jonah and his senior partners at Atlas Associates were ever mindful of the lines they couldn't cross in the office. But something about his tone and that wicked, predatory gleam in his intense gaze warned Denny that tonight was somehow different. *A birthday present?* What on earth was he talking about? There'd been no office birthday parties that day, and she remembered that Jonah had celebrated his birthday nearly three months ago.

Plus, how could someone actually *be* a present? Maybe if they were a stripper jumping out of some gaudy, oversized birthday cake. *No,* she thought with a soft, inner sigh of relief, Jonah surely wasn't asking her to do something like *that.*

But what is he asking me?

She watched with wide eyes as he reached out, and then *felt* as he smoothed one arched brown brow with the tip of his index finger. Her breath sucked in on a sharp gasp as he moved on to flick the tiny silver hoop pierced through the upper curve of her left ear, his blue eyes burning with a fierce, seductive heat that had a warm flash of pink climbing up her cheeks. Her female intuition was going on red alert as understanding dawned and she suddenly realized this wasn't just some sort of playful banter.

Crossing her suddenly nervous arms over her silk-covered chest, Denny tried to quell the flutter of butterflies in her belly. "Just what are you getting at, Mr. Cartwright?"

He gave her another one of those slow, sin-laced grins at the formal use of his last name, and that unhurried twisting of his wide mouth nearly—*oh so nearly*—made her moan with regret. If only she dreamed of this gorgeous stud the same way she did of his best friend.

His best friend…not to mention her damn boss.

Jonah was fine, no doubt about it, but it was Mr. Harrison, *Gabriel*, who made her ache with churning, desperate, lust-filled hope that a miracle would be granted and the one man she wanted for her own would someday wake up and finally take an interest in her.

Well, an interest that went further than what she ordered for lunch, she silently grumbled.

She was captivated by the wicked grin that curled the edges of Jonah's beautiful mouth, suggestive and teasing, and her pulse quickened, despite the knowledge that he was just toying with her. *He has to be. Right?* The guy could have any woman he wanted—*any woman*—and she was willing to bet her life savings that he had.

Moving that long-fingered hand across her cheek, he brushed a wayward strand of mahogany hair behind the shell of her ear, winking as he announced, "Today is Gabriel's birthday, Denny."

She cocked her head to the other side and blinked in surprise, wondering with heart-stopping expectation about his earlier opening statement. "He didn't mention it. *No one* mentioned it," she whispered lamely, nervously licking her bottom lip, her palms going damp when she saw Jonah follow the movement like an alley cat eyeing a slow, tasty meal of midnight mouse. "Er…how old is he?"

"Old enough, sweet stuff." The tall redhead's full smile flashed, as wickedly sinful as his reputation. For all of Gabriel's brooding darkness, Jonah was the epitome of the consummate devil, and a definite playboy. Hell, he'd even playfully flirted with her from time to time, but she'd never paid it much attention, and she'd never acted on it. Not that he wasn't a great guy, but she'd been pining away, like the lovesick idiot she'd become, for the one who made her heart shiver every time she set eyes on him.

Yeah, old enough, she silently snorted. *Lot of good it does me. Gabriel Harrison could be ninety and he still wouldn't want me.*

"And old enough to know what he wants," Jonah murmured, as if reading her mind. "Only a little too stubborn to go after it." He spread his arms wide, his dark sweater pulling taut across the solid muscles of his chest. At six-three, he was as tall and wide as Gabriel, and just as deadly when it came to masculine beauty and hard-edged sexual magnetism. "So, like any good pal, I'm here to get it for him."

Denny chewed her bottom lip, worrying away the cranberry gloss she'd applied during her last visit to the ladies' room. "And that would be what...exactly?" she asked with careful precision, almost afraid of what he'd say.

"A certain Miss Denny Abbott."

She couldn't help it—she snorted loudly this time. "Yeah, right."

Jonah clucked his tongue, giving her another playful wink. "I'm not teasing, Denny."

Without conscious thought, her eyes narrowed with beginning anger, even hurt, despite the unmistakable heat of anticipation racing through her veins. No matter how fiercely she might have wished it otherwise, men like Gabriel Harrison did *not* fall head over heels in love with women like her. Hell, they didn't even date them. They just stole their diet bars and drove them crazy with aching, unbearable longing.

"I'm sorry," she said tightly, her lips feeling strangely numb, "but I'm not as stupid as you obviously think I look."

"Cut the crap, Denny," he suddenly warned, brilliant blue eyes flashing with mild irritation at her words. "You know I think you're incredibly beautiful—inside and out—just like every other man who sets eyes on you."

As if, she silently laughed, wondering where he was going with this, but he only ignored her pointed look of disbelief. "If you trust me, you can have him. He's yours for the taking, sweet stuff."

Her heart dropped into her stomach with jolting, head-spinning speed. "Have...him?"

"Yeah," he said in that low, rough-velvet voice. "If you want it, you can have it all, Denny. Both of us can."

Both of us? Both!!!

"Just what do *you* get out of it?" she couldn't help but ask, still not really believing a word he'd said, though she was positive it'd be fueling her late night fantasies from here 'til kingdom come.

Before she realized what he intended, Jonah leaned down, braced his large hands on the padded arms of her chair, and pressed his warm, honey-flavored mouth against hers. With a rough sound of hunger, he slipped his talented tongue deep inside the warm recess of her mouth as she gasped in sudden, reeling shock against his silk-roughened lips. He tasted sexy and sinful, a heady combination that made her feel a little dizzy, as if her balance had been ripped from beneath her.

Ohmygod! It's a good thing my backside is still planted firmly in this chair, she mused in stunned disbelief, or she knew she'd have landed flat on her ass.

He took his time exploring the heat of her mouth, as if savoring what he found there, breathing into her until she felt drunk—even a little guilty with the flood of desire drenching her satin panties. Not that she owed Gabriel Harrison her self-imposed celibacy, but it felt somehow *wrong* to be kissing his best friend. Not to mention the fact that she was getting embarrassingly turned on in the process.

Nipping her bottom lip, Jonah pulled back, some of that teasing light replaced by a physical fire in his deep blue gaze that she could all but feel stroking her tender flesh, making her pussy swell with surprising need. "If this all goes to plan, then I get to enjoy the pleasure of this—of you," he rasped, rubbing her bottom lip with his thumb, "at least until Gabe kicks me to the street."

"*You want me to sleep with both of you?*" she nearly screeched, though she hoped the startled exclamation had actually come out as more of a hushed demand.

"I wouldn't put it quite like that," Jonah drawled, his heavy gaze burning with undeniable lust and humor.

"Yeah, then just how would you put it?" Denny muttered, shocked at herself for being so damned aroused by the idea. Reading about it in her steamier romance novels was one thing—but actually considering going to bed with two men at once went so far out of her comfort zone that she wasn't even sure it was in the same city. Not that she lived like a prude, damn it—but there was a world of difference between having had three lovers at different points in her life, all of them steady boyfriends, and fucking two drop-dead gorgeous business tycoons who probably made more in an hour than she did in an entire year, and who could both have their pick of the crop.

What in the hell are they doing going after me?

"I could put it a lot of ways," Jonah drawled, rising to stand before her, one big hand held out, tempting her to take hold—of him...of her dreams. Trusting him to lead her to *the one* she really wanted. The one she was uncomfortably certain—and absolutely terrified—that she'd love forever. "But one thing's for damn sure, Denny. For as long as Gabriel keeps me around, I sure as hell don't plan on letting you sleep."

* * * * *

Denny blinked slowly while drawing in an even slower, shallow breath, and looked around the opulent interior of the rapidly rising elevator, trying not to think about how insane this all was. The ride to Gabriel's apartment in Jonah's sleek little Audi had been too full of stunning revelations as she'd hung onto his every word, while he'd reluctantly talked of Gabriel's past, to think about how little she had in common with these two powerful men. The warm leather interior had teased her senses, soft beneath her body, tempting to her nose, the powerful purr of the engine exciting to feel—but it was the dark, rasping rumble of Jonah's words that had enthralled her.

The drive was short, but she'd been given her first little glimpse into the heart of the man she ached for as Jonah had answered her questions about his best friend over the steady rhythm of the tires upon the road and the low jazz playing through the smooth sound system. At the time, she'd been too interested in what he had to say to gawk at the unfamiliar luxuries surrounding her, but now she cringed at the obvious signs of wealth and prestige. From the gleaming parquet floor beneath her "red-tag sale" shoes, to the gilded mirrors reflecting her stunned, somehow haunted expression back at her a hundred times over—wide-eyed image reflected upon image in a dizzying, endless procession. It was suddenly more obvious than ever that there was more than just a world of difference between her and Gabriel Harrison. Hell, she was homemade fried chicken and mashed potatoes, while he was caviar and *Cristal* champagne.

No, not just a world—an entire freaking galaxy.

"Oh my God," she groaned under her breath, clutching onto the brass handrail at her side. At least she hoped it was brass. Damn, what if it was gold? *Gold freaking handrails.* A small, hysterical little laugh escaped her throat as she swallowed, determined not to let the panic bubble over. It would be too embarrassing if she started to hyperventilate. She licked her lips in a nervous gesture, the familiar taste of her cranberry gloss somehow comforting in the bizarre scheme of things, like a little scrap of home that she could hold close to her. "Explain to me again why I'm doing this?"

She scowled at the whispery thread of her words, but then Jonah's voice came strong and confident at her back, while the posh elevator continued to soundlessly hum its way up to Gabe's high-rise apartment, and she let herself get lost in his spell.

"Because you're in love with him," he rumbled, the smoky rasp of his shocking words falling over her shoulders like dark silk, calming her fears with the dangerous power of truth. They tempted her to forget who she was, who she'd been, and leap into a new, exotic, exciting skin of her own choosing. Tempted her to forget that middle-class, average-looking good girls didn't go to million-dollar bachelor pads and let their staggeringly sexy bosses fuck them silly.

A muffled kind of gasp trembled out on the dying edges of her laughter. "And how do you know it isn't just lust, Mr. Cartwright...er, I mean...Jonah?"

There was that wicked amusement again as he grinned at her reflection, reminding her that she was still calling the man by his last name, even though she planned on getting down and dirty with him before the night was through. Hell, maybe even within the next fifteen minutes. Who knew what kind of timeline these things played out on? Where was a bloody sex manual—*Ménage a Trois 101 and Other Helpful Hints for the Sexually Repressed*—when you needed it?

Damn. She couldn't believe she was actually doing this!

Strong hands moved to the back of her neck, kneading the tight, tension-drawn muscles, urging her to relax as the heady warmth of his skin eased into her, the slight calluses rubbing her tender flesh, making her think of how they would feel stroking across her nipples, cupping her mound.

With his breath warm and tempting at her nape, he murmured to her in an almost sad...solemn voice. "I know it isn't just lust, because whenever you set eyes on him, your pulse quickens and you have this tearing little ache in your heart, Denny. I've seen it happen. Seen it in your expression, in your eyes. It hurts, because you don't think you'll ever have Gabe for your own, the way you want him. That's how I know it isn't just lust. You look at me and you think *sure, he'd be fun to fuck*, but you look at Gabriel, and those sad brown eyes of yours burn with it, Denny. They burn with love, and it terrifies the hell out of him—almost as much as it makes him ache."

Denny turned her head sharply to stare over her shoulder and look at the man who was ripping open her soul. With wide eyes, she really *looked* at Jonah Cartwright for the first time ever, awareness hitting her with a jarring stab of understanding. His gaze held that burning flame of lust from before, but...there was more there. Pain? Loneliness? Hope? They all churned to life there in the sky-kissed depths of his eyes, the blue so crystal and clear it shared the beauty of a rain-splashed heaven, and she recognized just how unfair she'd been. Jonah might be a playboy, but there was a hell of a lot more to the man buried behind the gorgeous facade, if you took the time to look. Problem was, most women never got past the bad boy looks and heady edge of danger he wore like a second skin to see what lived beneath.

But if you looked—really took the time to *look* into the man—it was all there, as beautiful and pure as it was intoxicating.

"Relax and enjoy, Denny. God knows I am. I'd be willing to bet my life this is the last time I'll be so lucky with a certain little sexy brunette," he rumbled with a slow, teasing wink, as if he could sense her seeing into his soul and needed to lighten the moment, taking them back to easy ground. Well, easy for him maybe, she inwardly sighed, knowing that every step she took away from this elevator was going to lead her one step closer to paradise and hell. It all depended on how you looked at what she'd be going home with come morning.

Would the pleasure be enough to counteract the heartache? "You're crazy," she argued, worrying the fleshy part of her lower lip between her teeth, the taste of Jonah's earlier kiss a sweet, teasing memory upon its slick surface. "There's no way it will ever work. God, he's probably going to slam the door in our faces. And…and even if he does let us in, Mr. Harrison couldn't care less who I…uh, you know…fool around with."

"Not true, beautiful." His white teeth flashed in the soft lighting, the blue depths of his eyes hypnotically bright. "So not true, and there won't be anything *foolish* about it," he murmured, staring fixedly at her mouth until the moisture began pooling between the creamy lips of her pussy, wetting her panties 'til she could feel her warm wetness on the insides of her thighs, slippery and thrilling, like a naughty secret she couldn't wait to share.

She closed her eyes and bit back a groan, before opening them again and retaking his tender gaze. "Jonah, I can't help but be curious as to why you're so…uh, chipper about all of this?" Not that chipper was even close to the right word. No— he looked preternaturally hungry, as if lust were just oozing from his pores. Like he wanted to eat her alive, but make her smile while doing it.

One auburn brow arched in sensual amusement, the corner of his mouth kicking up with decidedly wicked purpose. "Do you really have to ask?"

Her eyes narrowed at his tone. "It's just, I mean, you're not *really* interested in me." No, that she couldn't believe—that two men wanted her for more than just sex. Hell, she was still having trouble believing the sex part, even after that toe-curling kiss he'd planted on her back in her office.

"Oh sweetheart," he drawled, trailing one big, rough palm down her arm to catch and squeeze her cold hand, "I know I'm not the one for you, no matter how much I might wish it otherwise." He turned her toward him and leaned his shoulder against the mirror at his left, then let those hungry blue eyes travel down her trembling length in a purely appreciative, carnal caress that spoke of primitive sex, sweat-slick bodies, and warm, tangled sheets. "But that doesn't mean I haven't had a good time thinking about what a hot little fuck you must be, more times than I care to remember."

Coming from another man, those words might have seemed insulting—but from Jonah Cartwright's lips, they sounded wonderfully sexy. "Sure you have," she chuckled, oddly comforted by his questionable honesty.

He nodded slowly beneath the golden light—shimmering, incandescent sparks of crimson color dancing through the auburn silk of his hair. "Since the moment I set eyes on you, in fact. Of course, Gabe nearly knocked my teeth down my throat when he caught me checking out your ass," he added with that mischief-made grin of his. "And then, later, once I'd seen the heat between the two of you, felt the tension, I knew that you were meant to be his."

"And you really think he'll want me, after I've...after I've fucked his best friend?" she forced herself to say, though the words felt forbidden coming out of her throat. Stiff and unsure.

"Ahh...but you'll be fucking him too," Jonah laughed softly, stroking his wide hand over the curve of her hip, those blue eyes moving with a slow, sensual urgency over her skirt-covered thighs, her belly, then lower, sending another flood of moisture to bathe her panties, soaking them through. "I think he'll want it, because he'll think it's safe. He'll see this as the way to get you beneath him, right where he's wanted you, and yet not have to give over his heart, the way he fears."

Denny cocked her head to the side, studying him as she let the words wash into her own fearful heart. "And what makes you think that's not precisely what will happen?" In which case she'd have one hell of an incredible memory to visit again and again during the lonely years of life ahead of her—but no Gabriel.

The elevator dinged to a slow, smooth stop, and Jonah led her into the polished hallway, that small, eager smile playing again at the sensual line of his lips. He stopped before the large ebony door on their left, and leaned down to place a teasing kiss at the corner of her mouth, then treated himself to a slow, tasting lick of her bottom lip. The musky male scent of his skin seeped through her pores, into her blood, and she felt that provocative lick all the way down to her toes, as if he were running that wicked tongue through the plump folds of her pussy instead. His breath quickened against her face as he stared down at her — her heart beating a resounding rhythm of terror and thundering need within her tight chest — and she watched with wild eyes as he drew a long white sash out of his pocket and moved behind her. Silencing her start with a warm finger across her quivering lips, he lifted the strip of satin to her already closing lids. She licked her lips again, ready to submit to wherever he would lead — and prayed like crazy that Gabriel would be there to catch her in the end.

"Gabe will give over his heart, because once he gets his dick in you," Jonah whispered roughly in her ear, his strong hands gently tying the silk off at the back of her head, "once he buries himself up your sweet cunt and feels you come apart around him, he'll know that he can't fight it any longer." A rough, boyish chuckle burst past his lips, and she smiled despite her nervousness and exhilaration. "And that's just about the time I expect to get my ass kicked out, with a rather explicit warning to never lay so much as a finger on you again. I've a feeling it won't take long for ol' Gabe to admit he's mighty possessive about you, Denny Abbott."

Taking her hand, he threaded his fingers with her own, wrapping his strong arms around her so that their hands rested against the gentle curve of her belly, her back to his hard-muscled front. He pulled her close, nestling what felt like a stunningly huge erection in the small of her back, and she could hear the smile as he said, "He'll know that in the end, we've no choice but to follow our hearts, Denny. Are you ready to follow yours?"

Am I?

She'd always chosen the safe guys. Chosen the guys she knew she could handle, only to have them bore the hell out of her. A little warning voice screamed from the region of her heart that this was a dangerous move—that she would be walking into that apartment, into the arms of Gabriel Harrison, expecting a hell of a lot more than she'd be leaving with. So she did what she knew she had to do. She hardened her jaw and told that damn voice to shut the hell up. If this was all she could have—a few mind-shattering hours of pleasure beneath the hands of the man she wanted, beneath the hands of two men who were the most gorgeous, virile, intoxicating specimens of raw sexuality she'd ever encountered—then she was going to take them.

Damn it, she *deserved* them. She deserved them for all the grunting, sweating, less-than-satisfactory hours she'd forced her body to lie beneath lovers who were so much less than what she hungered for. For the years she'd tried to convince herself that her wants were somehow skewed. That she was being unreasonable...too wonderfully unrealistic. So she'd tried to settle and stick, only to realize that in the end, she'd rather do without and take the edge off herself.

And if it was lonely with her vibrator and small, slender fingers, her dreams did what they could to quench the thirst for the taste of the forbidden that she craved.

She might be a nice girl. Might look like the kind of girl you wouldn't think twice about taking home to meet mom, but that didn't stop her from wanting to be the one who inspired fantasies. She wanted to be the one who could make a man— *her* man—go hard with little more than a look. Wanted to know the thrill of pushing him to the edge. Wanted to be able to pull the animal out of him, and feel the rush of being at the mercy of his raw, masculine hunger. The kind of primal hunger that was sharp-edged and jagged, overwhelming in its intensity.

And no one seemed more capable of showing her that than Gabriel Harrison—of giving her the physical, as well as the emotional release that she craved.

Oh, she knew she'd enjoy what Jonah could give her. Hell, it'd probably blow her mind—but Gabriel had the power to blow her heart. Her soul. He had the power to flow inside and become part of her. Not just her body. *Her.* To get down to what made her tick, and claim it for his own…if he wanted.

It was all his for the taking.

She was all his for the taking.

Her lips trembled, but her voice was strong and certain. The voice of a woman ready to walk out on the edge and grab life in a way she'd never had the courage to do before. Fearless and bold…*and by the balls.* "Yes, I'm ready, Jonah."

"Then let's do it, sweet stuff." And he raised their entwined fingers to knock on Gabriel's door.

Chapter Three

ಬಂ

The warm Scotch smoothed down Gabriel Harrison's throat as he took a hard swallow, like liquid velvet laced with sin, soothing and mellow, while the corners of his wide mouth curved with a questioning frown at the unexpected sound of a knock upon his front door. He set down his half-empty glass of *Chivas*, neat, as the knocking came again, his frown deepening until frustrated grooves bracketed his mouth. The scar on the left side of his upper lip pulled tight with his annoyed expression, a constant reminder of his failures in life. It was a maudlin fucking thought, he knew, but then he figured a birthday spent alone was as good a time as any to feel like shit.

The knocking came again, louder this time, insistent and sure, demanding his attention. He ran one hand through the thick, short black hair he kept cropped close to avoid the hassle of trying to control it, and used the other to set aside the latest paperback thriller he'd been doing little more than staring at. Thoughts still a million miles away, he stood up and winced as he felt the ligaments in his left knee twist into a wicked knot of pain—and tried not to think about the painful emptiness burning in his gut, keeping company with the Scotch.

Wondering who the hell was bothering him, he wrenched open the door and felt everything in his body come to a sudden, jarring stop—lungs, pulse, reasoning—they all came to a crashing stillness as if hurtled against the unforgiving surface of a brick wall.

He took in the couple standing before him, muscles seizing in a wrenching jolt of pure, unadulterated shock—and for the first time in years, he was completely speechless. But it wasn't from a lack of words, or things to say. No, too many words and curses crowded into his tight throat for him to choke out a single one. They lodged, hard and immovable, leaving him standing there, narrow-eyed and stiff as he stared at the way his best friend had his big hands entwined with Denny Abbott's feminine little fingers, and his strong, unyielding arms wrapped around her soft, womanly middle.

He was holding her.

Jonah is holding Denny, he repeated numbly to himself, something tight and suffocating churning in his stomach.

My Denny.

"Happy birthday, Gabe," Jonah drawled with a knowing grin, as if he *knew* just what the sight of them together, so comfortable and close, was doing to his gut.

Shit.

Denny gave a soft, almost inaudible gasp at the mention of his name, and Jonah's arms tightened around her, his mouth moving to the tender side of her neck, nibbling on her creamy skin in soothing encouragement. Gabriel watched the way he moved his lips against that soft, silky flesh, and felt a force move through him that had nothing to do with friendship, and everything to do with possession, primal and raw and bloodthirsty. A red haze burned at the edges of his vision, while the frigid chill he carried these days snaked deeper inside of him like an insidious sickness. Hell, it'd have been a big enough shock just to see Denny Abbott standing at his door, but blindfolded and in the arms of his best friend was about to fucking kill him.

As if a knife weren't being stabbed between his ribs, Jonah winked at him and said, "You gonna invite us in?"

Gabriel felt his glacial gaze drop to the thick arms wrapped beneath Denny's breasts, pushing the soft mounds up, her dainty nipples sticking out like hard little points beneath the silky covering of her blouse. Her scent—that luscious fragrance of jasmine and warm, moist female skin slammed into his senses, sending him reeling with an emotional punch that twisted inside of him, painful and tearing. His lungs burned, his heart pounded—and he didn't even want to think about his cock. It throbbed behind his fly, demanding and proud, uncaring that a wave of ice was crashing down over his head, trickling through his veins. A cold river of apathy that struggled to sweep him along in its churning, frigid wake, slowly deadening his senses, until he knew that one day there'd be nothing left to *feel*. Just a bitter, calculated landscape where emotions and guilt, dreams and hunger no longer existed.

And the only thing that kept him from becoming lost in that barren, desolate reality stood right in front of him, in the arms of another man.

Forcing his brow to arch in a casual expression of disinterest that was far from how he felt, he shrugged his wide shoulders, then leaned against the door frame, crossing his arms over the crisp white cotton of his shirt-covered chest, the sleeves rolled up casually on his thick, tan forearms.

"You sure you want me to do that, Jonah?" he rumbled, the husky baritone of his voice pulling another soft gasp from Denny. A gasp he would have liked nothing more than to feel against his mouth, teasing across his greedy flesh, soothing as it nestled against his scarred, hungry soul. "Looks like you and Miss Abbott are doing just fine on your own out there."

The corners of Denny's mouth quivered again at his words, but Jonah's smile only broadened, looking like a shark zeroing in on the scent of fresh blood. "Come on, Gabe. Invite us in. Denny and I can't give you our present out here in the hallway, man."

"What the hell kind of game are you playing, Jonah?" His words cut out of his mouth like the startling lash of a whip before he could curb them, sharp and stinging. For a moment, she looked so lost beneath the white sheen of the blindfold, even vulnerable, and he almost winced at her reaction to his anger, but caught himself, arguing an internal battle with his conscience.

Christ, what the hell had she been expecting? Open arms and a smile? Didn't she know better than to tempt him by showing up on his doorstep like a lamb being led to slaughter, leaving the safety and security of their impersonal working relationship so far behind?

And Jonah just kept smiling—that same wicked smile that always meant he was up to no good. "Thought I'd bring you a special present this year. A man only turns thirty-five once, Gabe."

"Thirty-five. Hell, is that all?" He felt ancient, like a fucking relic, something too old to be saved. "And call me skeptical, pal, but she doesn't look like a present."

"She's got the sash. I think that'll count." Jonah's wide shoulders shrugged in a casual gesture, the twinkle in his laughing blue eyes brighter than ever while the hallway lay in shadowed silence behind them—a sharp sense of anticipation lurking in its quiet emptiness, as if invisible eyes looked on with avid interest to see how this little scenario would play out. "Or would you rather I strip her and tie her up with a big red bow?"

"Would she let you if you tried?" Gabriel asked in a hoarse whisper, a taut, choking band of pained excitement tightening around his chest, stunning him. Here was his dream woman—with his best friend—offering what exactly? A fuck-fest? A little triple play guaranteed to shatter his sanity?

That cold, calculating part of his soul shouted that it was a dangerous move, but hell, how emotional could a friggin' three-way get? With Jonah screwing her alongside him, it wasn't as if his foolish heart could go off entertaining thoughts of dreams and romance.

Shit, for all he knew, she was there solely *because of* Jonah...and he was just an extra cock to get her off tonight. But damn it, that didn't sound like his Denny. Not that any of this struck him as something that could've been pulled out of her sexual repertoire. Denny Abbott was one of those rare women who made a man — the right man — think of *happily ever after* and *'til death do us part.*

"Would she let me tie her up for you? I think you'll be pleasantly surprised at what Denny's willing to do for *you*, Gabe," Jonah laughed, his look saying he knew "pleasantly" didn't come close to describing how he was really feeling. "And if you'd move your ass to let us by, she could prove it to you."

Huh — so this was all about him, was it? A goddamn birthday present guaranteed to knock him on his ass if there ever was one.

When he didn't make an immediate move to step aside and allow them in, Jonah feigned a hurt look of surprise. "Come on, man. Don't you trust me?"

Gabriel snorted. "Not fucking likely."

"Now that hurts, Gabe," Jonah sighed dramatically, shaking his head. "To think that my best friend, the man who knows me better than any other soul on Earth, doesn't trust me. I'm crushed."

"Huh...it's because I know you so well, buddy, that I *know* better than to trust your devious ass when you've got that look in your eye."

Jonah winced, saying, "Ouch," then smiled and gave Denny a quick hug that jostled her gorgeous tits, while a soft, nervous squeak slipped past her lips. With his chin planted playfully on her shoulder, Jonah laughed and said, "Then I guess you'll just have to trust Denny."

Gabriel watched as Jonah's hands splayed wide over her abdomen, one moving up beneath those luscious, quivering breasts, the other lowering so that the tip of his pinkie finger rested just above her skirt-covered mound. He swallowed, hard, knowing that the roaring in his ears his own goddamn pounding heartbeat.

"You do trust Denny, don't ya, Gabe?" Jonah pressed, rocking into the back of her body with a playful, suggestive motion that Gabriel knew was meant to drive him mad.

He opened his mouth, but any arguments or smartass comebacks he'd meant to make just stuck in his throat, leaving him sucking air. With a low grunt, he slammed his jaws shut, refusing to say a goddamn thing.

"Invite us in, Gabe," Jonah murmured, the cunning smile dimming across his mouth as he nodded toward the inviting room behind Gabriel's shoulder. "I can guarantee you won't regret it."

"Whatever, man," he finally grunted, moving back to allow them into the low-lighted room, then shutting the door with an ominous-sounding thud that vibrated down his spine. A fire crackled in the stone-front corner fireplace, filling the warm air with the burning, woodsy scent of oak and cedar, the reading lamp beside the sofa where he'd been sitting casting a glimmering, golden glow across the dark teak furnishings and plush Oriental carpets scattered over gleaming hardwood floors.

"Makes no difference to me if you want to put on a show. Gotta admit though," he muttered, forcing the words past the tightness of his throat, "I never really saw this as Miss Abbott's style."

"Yeah, well, you seem to overlook a lot of things these days, Gabe."

The words left Jonah's lips with a heavy drawl of satisfaction, as if breaching the doorway had been an act of triumph. From the corner of his eye, Gabriel watched Jonah lift the heavy, silken wash of Denny's dark hair, sifting the long mahogany strands through his fingers, watching the sensual dance of the firelight shimmer through the deeper red of the warm, rich browns. His fingers twitched, a restless, involuntary movement. He wanted to be the one playing with that gorgeous hair, feeling it slide across his skin, wrapping the thick, silky locks around the hungry dominance of his fist.

A heavy pulse of twisting, voluptuous need flooded his system, and for a moment he lost himself, standing there like a dumb-ass, staring at the fall of her hair over one softly rounded shoulder, as if it were a Renaissance masterpiece — before realizing that Jonah was still talking to him.

"Never know what you might miss, Gabe, if you don't look close enough to see what's really there. And if you're not careful, the things you try to ignore just might turn around and bite you in the ass."

"You switch sides without telling me, Jonah?" he taunted with a hard smile. "I wasn't aware you enjoyed biting guys' asses these days."

"Nice try," Jonah snorted, wrapping Denny back up in a tight hug, "but you can't bullshit with us, Gabe. Denny and I know you too well. You can try to get ugly, but we'll just see right through it. And we can be real pit bulls if we need to be. Tenacious as hell. Keep digging until we get down to all the really good stuff."

Christ, what is he going on about now?

It all seemed surreal as Gabriel stalked past them to the sofa, ignoring the screaming in his knee, trying to go for unaffected even though he knew — fucking *knew* from that look in Jonah's eye that the bastard had him pegged. How the hell had he given himself away? Jonah had always been an insightful son of a bitch, which made him so damn good in business, but now it seemed he was trying his hand at some kind of demented matchmaking scheme.

God save me.

Gabriel sat down and put his forearms on his spread knees, hands loosely clasped as he struggled to hold himself together. For a second, his gaze was drawn to the book lying at his right, while he tried to look anywhere but at Denny, as Jonah guided her further into the room ahead of him. The corners of his mouth shifted into a tight grimace, the novel striking him as a stark reminder of how he'd taken to spending his evenings. Bit by bit, he was withdrawing from everyone.

Everything. Was that what had prompted Jonah to bring Denny Abbott there tonight? Was Jonah going to use his one weakness to try and break through the wall of ice growing heavy and fierce around his heart, choking off his soul?

Hell, if anyone could do it, it was Denny. And he hated it. Hated the way he felt about her. Hated it as much as he craved being near her. So ripped open and raw, like a bleeding wound that only she could heal.

Forcing himself to lean back against the soft leather of the caramel-colored sofa, Gabriel ran one hand through the short, thick waves of his hair and tried not to groan at the too-tempting sight of her. Breathless, powerful visions of all the ways he could take her, dominate her, screw her beautiful little brains out, tumbled over one another in his mind in a helpless procession, like a taunting visual whose sole purpose lay in making him crazed. In tempting him to do the unthinkable.

They were dangerous visions—more so because they gained birth from his heart as much as from the aching column of flesh throbbing behind the buttons of his fly. "Enough of the bullshit, Jonah. What's she really doing here?"

One auburn brow arched above laughing blue eyes. "Isn't it obvious?"

Ignoring the telltale throbbing of the vein in his temple, Gabriel reached for the *Chivas* and downed the last swallow, a blistering scowl pulling his lips back over his teeth as the smoky amber liquid blazed a fiery path down his throat. The glass made contact with the end table in a distinct crack of heavy glass against even heavier wood, and all the while he stared at them from beneath the shuttered lids of his narrowed gaze, his voice a rough rasp stroking over the delicate silence surrounding them. "No," he lied, "it isn't fucking obvious."

"Oh man, tell me you aren't that far gone," Jonah laughed. "I know you've been doing the monk thing recently, but damn, I'd think this one was a little too easy to figure out."

Gabriel watched the smug ass lower his head to Denny's ear, and in a loud whisper, he said, "Maybe we should go back out into the hall, sweet stuff, let me strip you down to that gorgeous, satin skin of yours, and try this again. Do you think the sight of your beautiful, naked tits and hot, wet little pussy would give him a clue?"

He grunted, ready to tell Jonah to go screw himself, when Denny gave a soft, shy, kind of husky laugh that stunned him silent. God, he loved her laugh. There were times when he'd find himself walking by her office for no other reason than the desperate hope that he might hear her laughing, cutting up with her friends. It was so feminine, yet throaty, like the kind of intimate laugh you'd hear between lovers.

Only…he never laughed with his lovers, if you could use such an intimate term for the women he fucked.

It was embarrassing, what that laugh could do to him. Made him feel like he was jacked up on adrenaline, ready to burst with the need for a hard, pounding, uncontrollable ride, preferably while he was buried as deep into Denny Abbott as he could possibly get. There were some women who couldn't take all of him, but the hard, pounding ache in his cock, all carnal instinct and raging hunger, told him that Denny would. She might scream and writhe and claw at him, but she wouldn't be happy until she'd taken every inch he had to give her, and the thought had him breaking out in a hot, shivering sweat. *Damn.*

"Then I need to hear it from her lips," he all but croaked, struggling for his voice. "Miss Abbott—*Denny*—has to be the one to tell me exactly why she's here."

He watched as Jonah's long fingers curled over the feminine slopes of Denny's silk-covered shoulders, kneading the tense muscles there until a low, panting, wanton purr whispered past those pink, tender looking lips. They were like a soft, damp heaven, and he knew they would taste of promises and passion, warmth and all those forbidden emotions he had to stay clear of. He just wanted to lose himself in their silken heat, more than he wanted to breathe—and in that moment, he knew he couldn't kiss her, couldn't touch his hungry mouth to hers and take everything he knew he would find there. If they stayed tonight, he could fuck her and eat her and make her come until she was liquid and boneless. Yes. *Hell, yes.* He could even shove his cock past those dewy, pansy-soft lips and come down her throat—but he couldn't lose himself in the desperate, vulnerable touch of his mouth against her own, or he'd never survive.

One of the logs in the grate suddenly split, crackling with a loud pop of sound, and he jerked, only to realize Jonah was talking to him.

"I don't think she can really answer that right now, Gabe. She seems a bit breathless," the laughing redhead grinned. "Maybe a little too excited."

"She's not the only one," Gabriel muttered, recalling the thick bulge that had tented the front of Jonah's slacks before he'd pulled Denny back in front of him.

"What'd you expect, man? She's hot as hell." There went that damn brow again, Jonah's blue eyes taking in the obvious sign of his own hard-on pounding beneath the rigid fly of his jeans.

A dangerous, serpent-like anger slithered through Gabriel's veins, one he fought to tamp down before it raged beyond his control. His eyes narrowed in dawning realization—one that ripped at his insides even as he struggled to remain indifferent.

"And I bet you'd know, wouldn't you, Jonah? Hell, from the look of things, I'm guessing you know just how hot Denny can be."

"I haven't fucked her," his best friend drawled with that wry, knowing smile that was beginning to annoy the hell out of him. Then it changed, and became one of pure, feral anticipation, wolfish and sure. "*Yet…*"

The single word hung heavy in the air, weighty with meaning. Rubbing one rough hand over his eyes, as if he could rub the tempting image of her away, Gabriel struggled to regain his footing, but it was impossible. Having her near, all the evocative sights and scents and textures of her lush female form lured him in more completely than *any* woman he'd ever known. She was ripe with the promise of ecstasy, awash with the smoldering burn of arousal, and he wanted to lose himself in her.

Shaking his head as if that would clear it from the thick, clinging webs of lust, he muttered the one thing he knew with any absolute certainty. "This is fucking insane."

For the first time since he'd opened the door, Jonah's gaze went hot and hard with serious purpose, a warning glint flashing in the deep sky-blue.

"Don't be a chicken shit, Gabe, because we both know that's not your style. Denny was brave enough to come here tonight to give you a birthday guaranteed to blow your mind. You actually gonna turn her down?"

He wanted to. God did he want to, because there was an angle here, he knew it—the setup too easy and clean—but he was too far gone on need and hunger to figure it out. Just the sight of her, panting and trembling beneath the erotic blindfold, made his gut ache, his cock throb harder than ever before, as if it would erupt from within the confines of his jeans in search of her heat. Even his head felt thick with lust, the air moving through his lungs a heavier mixture, like the dense, rich spill of blood gaining a thundering momentum through his veins. How in God's name was he supposed to think with his dream woman being offered up like a friggin' prize?

He *couldn't* think.

"You gonna pass up the gift of a lifetime, Gabe? Ultimate pleasure with no strings or obligations attached. Come on, man, I thought you were smarter than that."

"He *is* smarter than that," Denny suddenly whispered into the desire-scented air, the husky sound of her voice stroking over him like the teasing press of lips down his spine, sipping from his flesh. The tip of her tongue touched the bow of her upper lip, and Gabriel nearly groaned aloud at the provocative sight.

Shit! *Shit. Shit. Shit.*

He stared at that fuckable mouth and wanted to eat her alive. Suck and lick and nip at her like he was starved, thrusting his tongue into that sweet heaven and swallowing her cries as he drove himself into her, giving it to her as hard and deep as he could. Maybe he couldn't allow himself to kiss her, but he *would* have her sweet pussy and that mouth. He *would* sink inside those full, lush lips, wide enough for the brutal, taking thrust of a man's cock—for the thrust of *his* cock—without having to hurt her, and yet, still perfect enough to make for a nice, tight fit. He wanted to see those sexy sweet lips wrapped around his long, thick dick, stretched and pouting as he held her stare, gripped her head, and fucked that angelic little face that tortured his sleep night after night.

She never wore lipstick, just that sheer, rosy gloss that smelled like cranberries, and it drove him out of his mind.

"You heard the woman," Jonah laughed softly, giving her an encouraging hug, his arms wrapping back around her in a possessive hold, squeezing her back to his front. "Guess that means we're staying."

Gabriel bit back the sharp, sour-tasting retort on his tongue, and allowed his eyes the tour they'd been longing to take since he sat down and Jonah had directed her to the spot where they now stood, no more than a foot from his bent knees. His eyes moved hungrily over her sweetly curved body, from the cute little shoes on her tiny feet, up her softly curved calves and thighs, to the sensual curve of her hips hugged in the loose folds of her knee-length skirt. He paused for a moment over the gentle arc of her belly, wanting to nuzzle there with his lips and tongue, learning her taste and softness.

Then his gaze lifted and his damn cock nearly exploded from nothing more than seeing Jonah's long, dark fingers twisting open the top button of her blouse, then the next, and the next, the deep, shadowy cleavage between her round breasts slowly revealing itself as the fine material parted inch by inch.

Then Jonah's movements deliberately slowed, and impatience forced a growling command from Gabriel's throat that caught him completely off guard, the words sudden and raw in his throat. "You brought her here, Jonah. Don't even fucking think of stopping now."

Gabriel stared helplessly at the sight of her, jaw clenched, teeth ground together so hard they ached, and his heart felt like it would explode. Shatter from nothing more than the sight of those magnificent tits quivering beneath the lacy white perfection of her bra, nipples a blushing pink promise of indescribable pleasure. He wanted those swollen nipples in his mouth, at the mercy of his lips and tongue and teeth as he bit and suckled and stroked her to a wild, sobbing, shivering release. Wanted her screaming and clawing and crying *his* name. Wanted their delectable taste and velvety texture catalogued in his mind, all the physical sensory data imprinted permanently upon his memory—his to explore at will—to revisit again and again when this night was over and she was no longer his.

"Wouldn't dream of stopping," Jonah laughed, his own voice emerging gruff with lust and unmistakable excitement. "Where the fuck would the fun be in that? And you know how I am, Gabe. An irreverent ass like me can't deny himself a good time, and it sure as hell doesn't get any better than this."

Jonah flashed the same cocky smile he'd been wearing the first time Gabriel had met him back in high school, the two then gangly freshman forging an instant bond when they'd been put on a week's detention for fighting with a group of seniors at a Friday night football game. The fight had been about a girl, Gabriel remembered with a wry inner smile. An older girl who they'd both wanted—and who already had a boyfriend. A rather large one, if he recalled correctly. They had gotten their asses kicked, but the friendship born from that bruising event had lasted through thick and thin, and more girls than he cared to remember.

But none of them had ever affected him like this one.

"Shit," he cursed softly beneath his breath, stomach tight with anticipation, as Jonah's big hands finished with the last buttons of her blouse, pulling the silky panels wide while a clenching awareness joined the exhilarating scent of expectation drifting on the air, like the parting of a theater's heavy curtains on opening night, exposing her to his violent, greedy gaze. Denny's slim hands fluttered at her sides in a nervous gesture, as if she fought not to cover herself, her dainty pink tongue licking her bottom lip in an evocative caress that made him want to follow its seductive path with the hungry urgency of his own, even though he knew he couldn't do it.

He watched, held captive, as Jonah stared down over her shoulder, his rough palms skimming over the satiny skin of her abdomen, until those lush breasts filled his hands to overflowing. Her breath caught as her head fell back against Jonah's chest, spine arching with pleasure, a sharp little cry of erotic surprise breaking past her lips.

"Man, Gabe, she's so fucking beautiful," his best friend rasped in a low, hunger-filled voice that made him want to knock the man's grin down his throat.

"Uhh...thanks," Denny whispered with a shaky smile, pulling that beautiful bottom lip through her teeth.

"Anytime, sweet stuff. Anytime," Jonah rumbled, an added huskiness to his deep voice that told Gabriel just how badly he wanted her. "All you have to do is say the word, and I'll be your slave, Denny. I'll serve at your feet, and let you have your wicked way with me, however you want it. Whatever you need. Your call, beautiful."

"Yeah?" Gabriel growled, a white hot, sizzling blaze of possessive fury ripping through him at the thought. "You gonna take Denny to that club of yours and let her put on a show, Jonah? Let all those arrogant assholes get their kicks watching while you nail her?"

Jonah fought for his smile, and won, but his lids lowered over the hot flash of surprise in his eyes, and Gabriel knew he'd scored a direct hit by bringing up his friend's dark little secret.

"No," Jonah finally drawled, after a brief pause. "The thought never crossed my mind, Gabe." His eyes crinkled at the corners, smile slowly widening. "If you want me to be perfectly honest, pal, something tells me that Denny's more than woman enough to hold my interest all on her own. And unlike some people I know," he added, lifting his brows, "I'm man enough to admit it."

He blew out a sharp breath, determined to hold onto his temper. "Are you trying to piss me off?"

"Me?" Jonah snorted, never losing that cocky-ass grin. "Wouldn't dream of it. Why would I even bother, when I can be thinking about fucking this hot little goddess instead?"

Denny gave a soft, nervous laugh at Jonah's words, and it all suddenly hit Gabriel like a swinging baseball bat upside the head. His best friend wanted to have sex with Denny—not for some scheme or setup or simple lust—but because he *genuinely fucking wanted her*, and that right there made Gabriel want to knock in more than just the taunting bastard's teeth.

And yet, there was no doubting that he would accept their gift tonight, because it was all he could allow himself. A night in which he could feast on the carnal delights of her flesh and nothing more, the two of them forcing the pleasure on her with fierce, deliberate intent, until they were covered in her sticky sweet cum. Until *he* was full on the sexy sweet taste of the juices he could scent on the air as she shifted her thighs in an urgent, restless movement of feminine need. Until he'd soaked her into his pores and taken everything she had to give.

And all the while, Jonah's long fingers plucked playfully at her lace-covered nipples, those burning blue eyes daring him to reach out and take what he wanted.

"If we're doing this, if this is really what she wants, then get her the hell over here," Gabriel growled, surprising himself with the suddenly snarled direction—one of clear, concise command and immediate objective. "Bring her closer, Jonah, and show me *exactly* what she's offering."

Chapter Four

ဆ

Closer…closer…closer.

The rumbled word echoed within Denny's mind like the revolving notes of a seductive symphony, one played out upon the instrument of her body as Gabriel's dark voice caught her up in an intoxicating web of arousal. If Jonah's voice held the warm, sultry rasp of fall, then Gabriel's was the smoky heat of a harsh winter's night spent before the crackling burn of a forest-scented fire. Together, they played upon her senses until she felt each cell in her body undulate with need, sizzling with desire.

However wet she thought she'd been before was nothing compared to the drenched heat slipping from between her thighs while she stood shivering and blindfolded, Jonah Cartwright's wicked fingers teasing her nipples with ruthless skill, and Gabriel Harrison sitting before her, watching their every move. Watching her beneath Jonah's hands, as the man pulled an erotic series of soughing, gasping moans from her lips, those skilled hands wreaking havoc upon her sanity. In her mind's eye, she imagined Gabriel sitting there like a dark pasha she'd been brought to entertain, glowing in sensual heat, those cool gray eyes narrowed with a sharp, predatory alertness and warning hunger.

Her thoughts drifted back to the drive there in Jonah's car, his words spiraling through her mind as she absorbed their meaning.

"How did Mr. Harrison get his scars?" she'd asked, palms damp as she'd twisted them upon her lap in nervous anticipation, wrinkling her skirt.

His eyes had flicked to the rearview mirror, lips twisting with quiet regret. "Those are really stories for him to tell you, Denny."

"Won't ever happen," she'd sighed. "That man doesn't tell me *anything*. On Employee Appreciation Day, he had Lucas come down to tell me what a brilliant job I do for the company. All Gabriel does is stare at me with those cold gray eyes, studying me, like he's trying to solve a riddle."

"Or maybe like a kid eyeing the one thing he wants for Christmas, but knows he isn't going to get?"

"Ha! Only because he hasn't asked for it."

"And that's *only* because he doesn't think he deserves it—but he's *wanted* to ask. Hell, I wouldn't be surprised if he was ready to beg."

She'd laughed softy. "You're so beautifully delusional, Mr. Cartwright."

"Under the circumstances," he'd drawled, slanting her a sideways look, "I think maybe you should start calling me Jonah, sweet stuff."

"Ahh, right." She'd nodded, unable to hold in her smile at his silly nickname for her. "I'll try to remember that...Jonah."

"See how easy it is?"

She'd returned his grin. "Hmm...almost as easy as it would be for you to tell me about Mr. Harrison...I mean, *Gabriel*."

His deep, rich laughter had rung out, sensual and full of life. "Damn, you're sneaky, you know that?"

"I prefer to think of it as wily."

"Yeah, well, much as I'd like for you to understand why he's acted the way he has, Denny, he's a guy who holds his secrets close to his heart. I don't think there are many who know much about Gabe's past, 'cept for me, Nic, Jack and Lucas. There aren't many secrets kept amongst the five of us."

Shifting uncomfortably in her seat, she'd turned slightly toward him. "Including tonight?"

Jonah had slowed around a corner, and then accelerated until Denny was clutching onto the sides of her seat for support. "Naw," he'd drawled, that wicked twist of his lips returning, "a gentleman never kisses and tells."

"That might make me feel better," she'd murmured, narrowing her eyes on him, "if you weren't grinning like a wolf when you said it."

He'd shot her a quick, smiling look. "You've got me there, but I give you my word that neither Gabriel nor I would ever mention what's going to happen in that apartment tonight."

Her chin had lifted, hands settling back into her lap as they'd slowed for traffic. "Are you willing to swear on it?"

"You wouldn't dare," he'd growled playfully, lifting his hand from the gearshift to shield his cock.

"Okay, okay, you can lose the panicked look, but I expect something in return."

His big, long-fingered hand had moved erotically against his crotch, eyes on the road while an endearingly wicked grin had kicked up the corners of his mouth. "Oh, you'll be getting some *thing* in return, sweet stuff."

"So then at least give me a small piece of Gabriel's past before I walk into that apartment." Her voice had lost its laughter, turning shyly quiet in the warm, leather-scented darkness of the sleek car. "He's so difficult to figure out. It's like he tries to be so cold, but there are times—there are times I've caught him looking at me like he wants to…to…"

"Eat you alive?" Jonah had drawled, giving her another quick, encouraging look before turning those deep blue eyes back to the road.

She'd shaken her head, watching her fingers play nervously with the hem of her skirt. "I was thinking get inside my head—see what I'm thinking. But maybe he looks at *every* woman that way. Or maybe he just feels sorry for me, because

I've given myself away with the way *I* look at *him*." She'd lifted her head, turning to stare at Jonah in the slashing glow of the streetlights as they'd sped along the road, admiring the way the fleeting shafts of gold painted the auburn bronze of his hair as it fell against the beautifully carved planes of his face. "Even you've picked up on how I feel about him. It's easy to reason that Mr. Harrison, Gabriel, has too. And if he truly, honestly wants...tonight, then why never show it? Why act so cold, like he's afraid to even touch me? To even shake my hand?"

Jonah had taken a deep breath, and then slowly released it, one hand flexing on the black leather of the steering wheel, while the other curved around the gearshift, sliding the Audi into a higher gear. "Because he *is* afraid, Denny. All Gabe has allowed himself for the past thirteen years is a string of women who've meant nothing to him. The last woman, a girl really, he let himself get close to died, and Gabe blames himself for that."

"She died?" Denny had repeated softly, swallowing a lump of surprise in her throat. "Thirteen years—that would put you two in college. Was she his girlfriend? Why does he blame himself?"

The questions had tumbled over themselves in a breathless procession, until Jonah had reached out to squeeze her hands, giving them a gentle shake. "I can't tell you that, sweet stuff. That's going to be up to Gabe. But trust me when I tell you that it's nothing but a stubborn, misplaced sense of guilt that's kept him from reaching out for what he wants."

Trust me...

Jonah's murmured words fluttered through Denny's mind, settling her nerves, helping her to refocus on the here and now.

Her nostrils flared as she tried to pinpoint Gabriel's distinctive scent over that of Jonah's and the warm, spiraling drifts of smoldering wood. There...yes, right *there*. She licked her lips, took that rich male scent into her lungs, and held it.

Woodsy, musky male perfection, with a touch of fine tobacco and even finer Scotch. The masculine aromas flooded her body with a vicious stab of sexual appetite, plumping the lips of her pussy 'til they felt swollen and heavy, eager to be stretched and pulled wide, separated for anything—*anything* these two arrogantly dominant men wanted to do to her. She felt raw with the cravings, ripped open, as if the physical hunger screaming to life inside of her could be seen by their eyes, felt by their touch. As if those feelings could be molded and stroked into whatever seductive shape they chose to create with their wealth of sexual experience and expertise.

"Mmm…you smell delicious," she murmured, voice unusually thick, husky with desire.

"What?" she heard Gabriel ask with a sharp breath, while Jonah rumbled with silent laughter at her back. She felt like an idiot, but she didn't care. "Your scent. Not cologne—just the smell of your skin, the drink I heard you sit down a moment ago, all mixed in with a little tobacco and the crackling, burning wood. It's warm and pulsing, like the beat of a heart." She inhaled deeply, letting it saturate her senses. "Delicious."

She listened as Gabriel dragged in a ragged breath, groaning, "Christ," in that deep, rough voice of his, while Jonah rasped a hoarse, "Damn," against her shoulder. With his mouth pressed against the sensitive skin just inside the collar of her open blouse, she felt Jonah smile as he said, "You're good at this, sweet stuff."

Her mouth opened, a teasing reply poised on the tip of her tongue, but Gabriel spoke first.

"Get her the hell over here, Jonah," he rasped, and she could hear him moving, hear the quiet rustle of his clothing against the fabric of whatever furniture he was sitting on, directly in front of her. "I want her closer. *Now.*"

Closer.

That single word expressed precisely where she wanted—*needed*—to be, and Denny couldn't deny the thrilling relief she'd felt when Gabriel had finally spoken that wickedly sinful command.

It was the command of a man riding that fine line between want and possession—and more than anything in the world, Denny wanted him to cross that line. She wanted to be possessed. Wanted to be taken by the hunger and physical craving, at the mercy of its greedy demands, if only to forget for just a few moments that this was the only time she'd ever be this close to the man who'd so effortlessly stolen her heart.

At this moment, all she wanted was to ease the blaze he'd ignited within her womb—the one snaking through her blood, poisoning her with fiery need. As if that need were calling, demanding her attention, a low, keening cry whispered past her lips, and Jonah laughed softly in her ear, nibbling sweetly on her lobe. His strong hands moved in a sensual caress from her heavy, aching breasts, over her quivering abdomen, down to her hips as he gently nudged her forward with the exciting press of his groin against her back.

And just like that, she was *closer.*

Closer to Gabriel. She shifted her feet and her knee actually bumped against his hard-muscled thigh, pulling a guttural, animalistic sound from his throat.

Denny swallowed a combination of nerves and wild, turbulent arousal, a sensation of tumbling helplessly upon the churning waves of a storm washing through her system, firing her blood. She expected the thick red fluid to bubble within her veins any second now, the heat of her desire like a scorching inferno, searing from the swollen tips of her breasts down to the aching, sodden folds of her pussy.

As if he could sense the ache torturing her there, Jonah whispered her name in her ear, one rough palm smoothing over the waistband of her skirt, driving down in a warm path of sinful intent until his long fingers were curling between her quivering thighs, cupping her moist mound in a hot, hard hold. His breath sucked in sharply between his teeth, hissing in her ear, while a low growl rumbled up from his chest, vibrating against her back, and that huge, hard erection she'd heard so many office rumors about pressed firmly into her spine.

"Damn, Denny, you're soaking, baby," he rasped in a harsh burst of breath and words, his palm moving over her with the barest teasing friction, the slippery cream spilling from her pussy quickly soaking through her wet panties and flimsy skirt, moistening his skin.

"I know," she panted, wanting to pull up her skirt and force those wicked fingers deep inside of her. "I-I can't help it."

A harsh, ragged sound, somewhere between a laugh and a groan, rushed past Jonah's lips. "We don't want you to help it, Denny. We want you dripping in these sweet pussy juices, all slippery and slick, coming all over us. However wet and hot and hungry you get, it won't be enough, baby. We'll just keep pushing you, demanding more, until you give us everything. All of it."

"Oh God," she moaned, biting her lip to keep from crying out, her breath shuddering in her lungs. *Damn.* She was burning, pulsing and hot, the tender cushion of her pussy throbbing and wet, soaked with the steady flow of her juices. Warm and smooth, they slipped across the sensitive surface of her folds beneath the erotic press of Jonah's hand, and she could hear him—*Gabriel*. Hear the sudden, evocative whoosh of air as his breathing grew deep, heavy, rasping out over the breathless pant of her own.

Her heart jolted, and she licked her lips, the sensual smell of cranberry gloss filling her nose, while beneath that temptingly light fragrance pulsed the deeper, heavier, musky scent of male desire. Then Jonah flicked his thumb across the swollen nub of her cloth-covered clit, and she gasped, trembling. "Oh…oh, *shit*."

Silent laughter rumbled against her back. "Wow, Gabe. Did you hear that?" Jonah teased. "We made sweet little

Denny say a cuss word out loud. Damn, I bet we're heading straight to the seventh circle of hell for that one."

"Right," she snickered, shaking her head at his foolishness. "Like you two devils need any help from *me* to get there. I'm sure you've managed that just fine on your own. You probably already have adjoining suites, with your names charred into the doors, just waiting for you."

There was a strange, choked sound from Gabriel, as if he'd swallowed a bark of laughter, while Jonah chuckled in her ear. "I like seeing you loosen up," he laughed. "I wonder what else we can do to help you let loose and go wild?" She felt his head lift, and knew he was looking down at the man who sat before them, his big hand still rubbing against the drenched heat of her panties. "Wouldn't you like to watch Denny go wild, Gabe?"

"I'd like to watch her do anything," Gabriel said in a low, gritty voice, the words coarse and tight, as if he struggled not to say them, but couldn't hold them in. As if they were being pulled out of him against his will, and the thought gave her hope. Hope that together, she and Jonah were making a dent in that infuriating control of his.

"Well hell, that's pretty damn telling, wouldn't you say, Denny?" Jonah drawled with obvious satisfaction, grinding his palm against the pad of her pussy while his wicked thumb began to rub breathtaking circles into her clit.

"*Uhhmm,*" she moaned, not trusting her own voice at that moment. Not trusting what she'd say or shout, and partly terrified that she was going to start gushing like an emotional hose, begging and pleading and ruining everything. To stop herself, she bit down hard on the inside of her cheek, but there was no controlling the rapid, violent pounding of her heart that his words had caused.

Then the world was spinning as Jonah's strong hands turned her hips, bringing her around to face him. She bit her lip, orienting herself with her palms flat against the warm cashmere of his sweater, feeling the broad, solid, mouthwatering expanse of muscle tense beneath her touch.

With a soft, soothing murmur, as if he were gentling a frightened animal, he lowered her arms and smoothed her blouse off her shoulders, following the silken fabric as it slowly traveled the length of her arms, whispering against her skin, until he finally pulled it free from her wrists.

"Just making you more comfortable, sweet stuff."

"If only a girl had a dollar for every line she heard like that," Denny half-laughed, half-sobbed in a breathless rush of air. The lace-covered tips of her breasts pressed fully against his chest as he laughed, all that masculine tactile heat burning against her, as searing as the press of Gabriel's eyes against the vulnerable, naked line of her spine.

"Not a line, sweet stuff. I just want you to relax—let us make you feel good."

And it was like floating in a thick, hypnotic daze when she felt Jonah's face nuzzle her neck, nipping playfully at her skin, every touch, taste and scent electrified by the removal of her ability to see…to anticipate. Large hands settled again at her hips, grasping the fragile fabric of her skirt, and he began coiling the diaphanous length around his clenched fingers, while strange, incomprehensible little murmurs of desire drifted from her lips.

Her hemline lifted higher and higher, inching up the backs of her trembling thighs, until she felt it skim the generous globes of her bottom, gathering into the small of her lower back. Jonah pulled the cinched length of fabric to the side, securing it with one large hand, while the wicked fingers of the other slid over her satin-covered cheeks, the rough calluses she assumed he and Gabriel earned from all their weekend sailing snagging at the delicate fabric.

"Such a sweet, beautiful ass," he rumbled against her throat, long fingers kneading her flesh.

"Turn her around," Gabriel suddenly grunted, the rough, tangled sound of need in his harsh whisper pulling a whimper from her throat.

Jonah turned her in front of him until her back once again rested against his front, her head spinning while a jagged laugh burst from his throat—this time so different than before. With her skirt hiked up high to the side of her hips, Jonah didn't hesitate, delving straight into the sodden satin fabric of her panties.

"*Denny.*"

"*Uhhmm,*" she moaned again, responding to Jonah's husky voice growling her name by turning her face toward his, and then he was pressing the hot, rough-silk of his mouth against her own, his breath tempting and teasing, tongue tracing her lips in slow, lingering laps. For a moment his palm simply cupped her, as if holding in her heat, and then she felt him move those long, thick fingers through her folds, and her thoughts shattered into a million irretrievable pieces. With her head still spinning, heart pounding to a powerful cadence of pain-edged anticipation, she felt Jonah snag the soaked crotch of her panties with his fingers, then slowly, torturously, pull the drenched satin to the side, exposing all the naughty, wicked need of her pussy to the eyes of the man sitting before her.

Through ears thick with the powerful thundering of her pulse, she listened as Jonah said, "So tell me, Gabe, what kind of pussy does our sexy little Denny have?" His voice scraped with need, but she could hear the smile on those sinful lips as he rumbled, "I bet it's as gorgeous as the rest of her. I swear she's so hot and sweet, she's burning my hand."

Gabriel snarled a low, blistering curse in response to Jonah's taunting, and leaned forward, moving *closer*. Denny knew because she could *feel* his breath against the sensitive inner surfaces of her thighs, and every muscle from her toes to her temples clenched in sudden, reeling expectation. She couldn't see, but she could *sense* the press of his eyes upon her heated skin, the flesh tingling as if she were touching voltage.

"You should have offered me first feel, Jonah."

"Hell, and risk getting pushed out of here before I got to experience this?" Jonah snorted, lapping his tongue against the sensitive underside of her jaw, trailing it in a slow path down the tender side of her throat. "I don't think so, pal." His fingers drifted lower, through her slippery, swollen labia, circled her vulva and then flicked back up to twist playfully around the ripened nub of her clit. Then, as if losing patience with the clinging satin, he fisted his hand in the crotch and gave a vicious tug, then another at her hip, and the ruined panties floated down her legs, landing across the leather-covered toes of her left foot.

"Oh God," she croaked, stiffening her thighs, following Jonah's lead as he used his knee to edge them wider apart, until she was standing with her weight resting completely back upon his chest, legs spread within the frame of Gabriel's solid, immovable thighs, pussy naked and vulnerable to his intimate scrutiny.

"You know, I do believe she likes you, Gabe," Jonah drawled, slipping his fingers back across her intimate folds as her juices continued to run warm and free.

"What the hell do I have to do with it?" Gabriel muttered, the harsh breath of his words slapping against her skin, firing her pussy as if he'd tapped it with the flat of his palm. "You're the one fingering her ripe little cunt, Jonah."

And he was. Those questing fingers teased around her clit, then dipped lower again, petting the puffy lips until she couldn't control the fine tremor vibrating through her limbs. Her hands grasped the hard, unforgiving muscles of the arm holding her skirt in place, short nails digging into his skin until she knew she'd be leaving little crescents within his firm flesh.

"Ah," he drawled, resting his chin on her shoulder, "but I'd be willing to bet my life it's you she's thinking about right now, Gabe. Thinking about you looking at her, those cold gray eyes going hot with hunger, glued to the incredible sight of her cunt being pulled open, all her pretty little secrets revealed to you. She's watching you, Gabe, without even being able to see you. Imagining what you look like right now, what you're seeing, licking her lush lips with that pink little tongue, wondering what you'll taste like in her mouth. Bet it makes you feel as if she can see straight into your soul, doesn't it, man?"

Gabriel made another kind of indistinct, guttural sound, as if the situation had become too primitive for speech, and Jonah gave another wicked laugh, grinding his erection into her spine, reminding Denny that she was at the mercy of two consuming hungers here. Then he rimmed the tender edge of her vulva with the hot tip of one finger, and pushed the thick digit up into the grasping bite of her pussy. Instantly, everything inside of her clamped down so wonderfully hard, eager to keep him inside.

"Damn," he groaned, his long finger flexing, pumping its way through the silken walls of muscle as her pussy sucked him in, rippling with need. "Jesus—you gotta feel this, Gabe. Feel how tight and sweet this little cunt is."

The wicked words moved through Denny like the drugging flood of wine, heating her from the inside out, and then she couldn't feel anything but a searing, electrical shock of carnal pleasure as a second big, hot, hard hand moved between her legs, the rough, callused tip of a thick finger stroking softly at the edge of her vulva. It lingered there, exploring, sampling, before purposely, determinedly—since she was so tight and the fingers were so deliciously big— working its way up into the clenching wetness, giving her a full penetration.

Oh God, Gabriel had added his finger, joining Jonah's, as they pressed deeper within her pulsing slit, parting her walls, her tender vaginal tissues stretched to the point of burning, thick cream spilling from her womb, drenching them as her muscles seized down in an impossible hold meant to pull them even deeper. She tried to hold it back, to bask and writhe in the indescribable pleasure, but it was unstoppable, rushing over her like a wave of breathtaking, churning ecstasy. She came instantly, the raw carnality of having each of them inside of her, those thick fingers moving through the tender, tight clasp of her inner muscles, pulled the pleasure from her in a way that was simply too much to resist. It ripped up from her soul, clawing and violent, exploding from her womb as the roaring climax blazed over her before she could stop it, a wrenching, crying sob breaking from her open mouth, head thrown back against Jonah's chest as the spasms clenched deeper within, contracting her muscles, spilling her hot, thick juices until she knew their hands would be wet up to their wrists. Denny felt as if she'd become one single, drumming throb of sensation— something powerful and new rising from the seared ashes of the average woman she'd once been, transforming her into a creature who now, after having found what it craved, wanted it again….and again…and again.

Closer. More. Closer. More. Over and over, the insatiable demands fired through her blood, pumping with life, demanding satisfaction. Her hips rolled, lifting toward the harsh breath she could feel blasting from Gabriel's mouth, blowing against the smooth, bare lips of her pussy, through the tiny patch of brown curls she kept groomed at the top. Christ, she had to get *closer*.

Closer.

More.

Everything.

"Ah…damn," Jonah growled, nipping at her shoulder, "that was friggin' beautiful, Denny. Like holding a goddamn ball of flame in my hand, sweet stuff."

She opened her mouth, her skin going moist with a fine sheen of sweat, the damp hair at her temples catching at her cheek, and tried to respond, with what she didn't know. *Thank you? Again, please?* Hell, anything, but nothing could work its way up from her tight throat except rushing gasps for air as she struggled to feed oxygen into her starved lungs. And then she heard it, that single word that found its perfect match within her lust-drugged brain.

"*More*," Gabriel growled in a hoarse, ragged voice, like a man who'd struggled for an eternity to get to this moment in time, her pussy still rippling in telling little aftershocks around the thickness of their fingers. "*I need more. Now.*"

That was it. That—*that*—she needed to see. Gabriel taking more from her. Taking what he wanted—needed. With one trembling hand, Denny reached up and ripped the blindfold from her eyes, throwing it aimlessly to the side as she blinked rapidly against the golden light and lowered her gaze, locking it hungrily onto the man sitting before her, his long, hard body perched on the edge of a beautiful leather sofa. She swallowed at the sight of those mesmerizing, hypnotic, silver-flecked eyes burning up at her, the heat passing between them so intense she was amazed she didn't hear it crackle and sizzle on the softness of the air.

She wanted to throw herself at him and confess everything inside of her, but Denny knew the raw bones of the situation, no matter how prettily Jonah had tried to color it. This was about sex, at its rawest and most simple—but she was going to grab hold and dive in anyway, taking whatever measure of the man she could get.

Oh hell, who am I trying to fool?

She could talk a good game, but it didn't amount to a hill of beans. Standing before him, staring down into that fathomless gray gaze framed by beautiful thick black lashes, she knew her heart was far from being as protected as she'd hoped.

Can he really feel...something...for me? Do I dare let myself believe?

Gabriel blinked suddenly, breaking their connection with a small shake of his dark head, and for a moment his eyes narrowed on her with so much resentment and anger, it was as if he looked at her with accusation—as if he knew what she could see inside of him and was enraged with her perception. But then he blinked again, a slow, sensual shift of those long-lashed lids, and the hunger burned through brighter than ever. And in that moment, Denny knew this was *right*. Felt it with every facet of her being. Every cell. Every memory and the wistful hope for the future that lived in her blood and heart and thoughts, taking shape in her dreams.

Staring, she watched as Gabriel pulled carefully free of her body, then grasped Jonah's thick wrist in a tight hold, pulling his cream-covered finger from the snug clasp of her sex, the tender tissues making a little popping, slurping sound as the long digit pulled free. His hard look dared the other man to protest, but Jonah only smiled against the side of her neck, quickly unfastening her skirt, letting the soft cloth slip down her legs, before moving his hand under her right knee, his fingers wet against her skin, opening her a little farther. Gabriel's mysterious, undeniably sad gray eyes lowered and he tightened as if he'd been punched, every long, powerful muscle in that magnificent body going wire-tight with tension. His jaw worked, that telltale vein throbbing hypnotically in his temple, and then he groaned like a man starved for the taste of something he knew he could never have.

Denny watched, mesmerized, as Gabriel dragged his long, thick finger, the same one that had been inside of her, through her pussy-pink lips, the dark length gleaming wetly with her juices as it reached her slick, swollen vulva, circling the tiny pink rim with a delicate, teasing touch so at odds with his dark expression.

"You have such a beautiful cunt, Denny. Absolutely beautiful."

"Oh my God," she gasped, squeezing her eyes shut.

I want things moving quickly, Jonah had warned her on their way there, and God were they ever. She knew he wanted Gabriel *feeling*—wanted him riding on a fierce wave of arousal, emotion and need—not thinking and working everything through in that analytical brain of his. She had thought she was prepared, but she was still reeling from the speed with which this was all unfolding, feeling like a bumbling novice as she tried to keep up.

With a deep, shivering breath, Denny lifted her lashes, the salty sheen of moisture washing through her gaze softening the sharp, red-tinged angles of Gabriel's frustration. This right here—the threat of ultimate pleasure and sin—might be her only chance of ever breaking through to him. Of ever getting deep enough inside of him to discover the demons he kept hidden there and help him destroy them once and for all.

He suddenly looked back up at her face, and as if he could see inside her mind, reading her thoughts, his expression hardened with blistering emotion.

"Don't even try to go there, Denny," he warned. "Trust me—you won't like it."

She tilted her head to the side. "And how would you know what I like?"

He didn't answer, simply moved his hand to her thigh, fingers clenching around the giving flesh, and her eyes found another scar on his forearm, most likely from a knife. It cut across the dark beauty of his skin with its masculine covering of silky black hair, tapering off as it bisected the thick veins that crossed beneath the warm flesh on the tops of his large hands. She'd never seen him with his cuffs rolled up, and so she'd never before witnessed the angry evidence of this wound as it cut a jagged line up his arm. It seemed so impossible that Gabriel had ever suffered physical pain, and yet these scars were proof enough that someone had dared to do battle against him. Dared to pit themselves against all that lethal, intoxicating power held so casually, always so masterfully controlled by his will and personality. How much had that control cost him? What price had he paid for the cold mastery that now existed as so much a part of him?

Reaching out, Denny traced the raised line of flesh across the back of his hand with her fingertip, ignoring the way he flinched beneath her touch. "You're such a mystery, Gabriel. So many secrets hidden inside of you. So much you won't share."

She wanted to know...to learn all that there was inside of him, the good and the bad. All of him—God, she just wanted to take every part of him into her and hold on for always.

"Spread her wider," he suddenly ordered, as if she hadn't spoken, his voice once more sounding like the stinging lash of a whip. His nostrils flared, eyes blazing with a roiling gray flame that seemed to melt into her soul, everything deep inside of her lust-heavy body rushing in sexual frenzy. "Wider, Jonah. I want to see every pink little piece of this juicy cunt you've brought me."

"My pleasure, Gabe," Jonah drawled, smoothing his hand along her thigh as he pulled it up higher, out to her side, the conservative heel of her shoe catching on the gleaming teak of the coffee table at their right. He pulled a little more, until those puffy lips pulled open even wider, the glistening pink flesh inside hungry for anything...everything, while her juices dripped back into the crack of her ass. Gabriel studied her, those rough fingertips stroking, exploring across the folds of her pussy, every touch claiming just that much more of her, so that she felt branded with his possession.

She watched him follow the teasing trickle of her juices with those narrowed eyes, before catching them up with the tip of a finger, then rubbing the syrupy fluid between his thumb and the blunt digit. His mouth tightened, scar going white as the frustration thundering through him could all but be felt—heard—as it gathered with mounting force.

"Christ, you're such a bastard for doing this, Jonah. A miserable fucking bastard," he snarled in sudden, vicious accusation, and then he leaned forward and his face—Gabriel Harrison's hard, gorgeous face—shoved itself against the hot, pulsing cushion of her vagina, his tongue immediately stroking out to lick through her tender, liquid-soft folds.

A feral, beastly growl rumbled and lashed out from his throat, shuddering against her tingling flesh as he pulled back enough to cut his glittering gray gaze up to her face, his wet lip curling with obvious fury.

"You should've been smart and stayed the hell away from me, Denny. *I fucking warned you.* Every time I've ever set my goddamn eyes on you, you *knew* what I was warning you of."

"Yeah," she whispered, licking her lips, intoxicated by the look and feel of him, by watching him put his lips to her...*cunt*, as he'd called it, and lick her juices into that wicked mouth. She wanted *more*. Needed *more*. Needed more of the mind-shattering *pleasure*. Needed to be *closer*. Rolling her hips, Denny nudged her drenched sex against his rough chin, the dark stubble of his beard giving the wet flesh an erotic scratch of sensation.

"Go on, Gabriel," she rasped, letting go the slow, siren-born smile playing at her lips. "Warn me some more, gorgeous. I *dare* ya."

Chapter Five

ഇ

"That a girl, Denny," Jonah laughed. "Don't let him scare you, sweet stuff."

"He doesn't," she murmured with a wry twist to her lips, surprised at the steady tone of her voice. "Make me crazy, yes—but he doesn't scare me."

"Maybe you should learn to be more cautious," Gabriel grumbled, though an answering grin seemed to curl lazily at the hard edge of his mouth, a flicker of humor sparking for just a moment in his soft gray eyes. Her own eyes widened, going big and round at the sight. Amazing, how that brief flash of amusement dancing across his harsh features made her insides go all mushy and warm, like soft melted taffy on a moist summer day. She wanted to see it there again. Wanted to hear the sound of his laughter. Wanted to feel it rumble from his chest as he pressed her to his heart, those powerful, well-muscled arms holding her tight and secure.

It was a beautiful thought, leaving her adrift on the fluffy, cloud-like wisps of a daydream—then those rugged hands that had inspired so many of her naughty midnight fantasies lifted between her spread thighs, calloused thumbs stroking down the slick, swollen labia from top to back—and she couldn't think at all. Her mind went blank, and *feeling* became her focus. Once. Twice. On the third pass they pressed and pulled, opening her liquid center like the parting flesh of a peach as his thumbs pushed into the dripping, succulent fruit.

"Mmm…that's probably some good advice, only—I don't want to be cautious," she finally murmured, her words sounding thick with the pleasure she didn't even try to hide. Her head fell back against the solid wall of Jonah's chest, moving from side to side as she felt her hammering pulse not only in her veins, but across the surface of her skin, as if a thousand tickling licks of flame were dancing over her sensitized flesh.

"Christ, you're so beautiful," Gabriel groaned in a hard, heavy growl, all traces of humor vanquished beneath the carnal, clawing sound. A deep, dark animal growl that made her jolt in Jonah's strong, immovable arms. "Prettiest little damn pussy I've ever seen, Denny."

"I'm...um, glad that you like it," she moaned, knowing that she would remember this moment for the rest of her life. She forced her eyes open, unable to recall when they'd closed, and looked down to see that small, wicked grin playing once more at the corner of his hard mouth, head tilting ever so slightly to the side as he studied her.

"I don't just *like* it, angel." His expression pulled the small scar that slashed into his upper lip tight, and she swallowed another telling moan, feeling a swift, eager need raise its head within her, its sole desire to run her tongue over that marred flesh with a slow, tasting lick. She wanted to take that wounded part of his soul and lave it with the wet heat of her desire. Wanted him to know that she hungered and ached for every incredible inch of him. Not his money or his corporate power. Not the tactile wealth surrounding her or the sleek Porsche he kept parked downstairs in the private space she'd seen when Jonah parked his Audi.

No, she hungered for the man—the flesh and blood and bone—with a need that consumed her, eating at her from within.

Just like before, Jonah's words found their way back into her consciousness—those brief glimpses into Gabriel's soul that she'd consumed on their way there tonight, so eager to learn all that she could about the man who held her future without even knowing it.

Or maybe he did understand what he meant to her. Maybe that had been the problem all along.

"I still don't see why you can't tell me how he got the scars," she'd argued as Jonah had parked the Audi, unable to stop herself. "They couldn't have all happened in one night."

"Hell yes, they could have," he'd laughed, though the sound had been strained. Turning off the engine, he'd sat in the quiet darkness, blue gaze shuttered as he'd looked at her, shielding the mysterious expression in their dark depths. "When he was younger, Gabe had a hell of a temper, Denny. One that landed him in trouble with the governing board of our university and almost got him kicked out of school."

"He fought a lot," she'd murmured, trying to reconcile the man she knew who held his temper and emotions under such tight control, with the volatile, hotheaded youth he used to be.

"Yeah," Jonah had laughed softly, "that's one way of putting it. He didn't go out of his way to look for trouble, but he didn't walk away from a situation if it pissed him off either. His knee got screwed up the time he stepped in to help out this scrawny little freshman. Some older assholes were ganging up on the kid, and it got pretty ugly. Hell, I'd have been there at Gabe's side, like I usually was, but that morning I was still nursing a serious hangover from too much partying the night before," he finished with a wry twist of his lips.

She hadn't been able to help but smile at his expression, even while his words had soaked into her soul, filling in the needy spaces that hungered for answers and truths. "And the others?"

Shaking his head, he'd said, "The one you really want to know about—that painful bastard on his lip—that one happened the night Karen died, and you're going to have to make Gabe tell you about it, sweet stuff. I won't break his confidence."

"You're right," she'd nodded, blowing out a tense breath. "I wouldn't want you to. It's just—there's so much I don't know about him, and so much I want to understand."

"You will. By the time this night is over, I'd be willing to bet my life that Gabe will tell you anything you want to know, Denny. Just be...patient...with him. This is gonna hit him like a Mack truck, and knowing Gabe, he's gonna put up one hell of a fight."

But he wasn't fighting right now. Right now Gabriel Harrison was killing her with the pleasure that wicked mouth of his could deliver.

He leaned forward slowly, eyes snagging hers again as his tongue stretched out, stroking through her parted folds in a hot, lingering lick that started at her swollen clit and didn't end until he'd teasingly curled it around the shy, puckered entrance of her ass, tasting her completely. Denny made a strangled noise in her throat, but didn't—*couldn't*—break that demanding stare, not even to blink, as he stroked back up to the top of her slit and ever so slowly, deliberately, curled that wicked tongue around her now-throbbing, blushing clit. His warm, mobile lips pulled back over his straight, white teeth, then nipped, scraping gently over the sensitive, pulsing nub. A croaking sob spilled past her tingling lips, shocking her with the primitive sound of need—*of want*—being ripped up from her body, as if he were reaching down inside of her and pulling up the deep, dark desires she'd kept hidden so far within. Hidden so well, she'd refused to admit some of them, even to herself.

But right here, in this moment, Denny knew precisely what she wanted to experience beneath those dark, powerful hands and the strong, clever tongue playing over her pussy. She wanted to be taken, ravaged and devoured, damn it. Wanted to be held down while his hard, powerful body moved over her, within her, his heat and strength and raw, sharp-edged energy covering her like a storm, overpowering and beautiful in its intensity. She wanted it all. Every single mouthwatering, intoxicating pleasure that wickedly sinful gray gaze promised her.

And she didn't necessarily need to be taken with gentleness.

"You look so sexy," Jonah whispered in her ear, reaching down, shushing her when he gripped her other knee and she squealed, startled. He shifted, and she nearly squealed again as she found herself held—suspended against his body—his hands beneath both her knees, pulling her thighs outrageously wide. She scrambled for leverage, hooking her arms back behind his powerful neck as she struggled not to feel foolish, held and spread before Gabriel, the moist, juice-slicked folds of her vagina wide open and ripe for the taking.

But if her position felt ignominious, Gabriel certainly seemed to like it. He growled another menacing sound of need in the back of his throat, lowering his head as he suddenly pressed his face deep into her giving flesh, and all she could do was stare down at him in helpless pleasure and rapt fascination, utterly at his mercy as he began to give her the sexiest, rawest, naughtiest tongue fuck she'd ever experienced. His mouth was avid in its quest, lips and tongue and teeth all working as instruments of sensual torture as he stroked and suckled, the hungry snarls of sound breaking from his throat vibrating against her pulsing flesh.

"*Oh god, oh god, oh god,*" she chanted in helpless revelry, entirely at the mercy of the sinful sensations coursing through her blood. A heavy, wicked pressure built from within, and she wondered how she didn't just come apart at the seams, shattering beneath the thrill of his mouth eating at her like a man starved for the taste of life.

"Watch him," Jonah whispered, licking her ear, nibbling on her throat as he pulled her knees higher, tilting her pelvis into Gabriel's face.

That gray gaze dared her to do as Jonah said as he pushed the scraping flesh of his tongue into the snug clasp of her tender opening. Then one wet thumb dipped lower, pressing just inside the impossibly tight, sensitive ring of her ass, and it shocked a raw, hoarse cry from her throat. She'd never been touched like that *there,* and it felt as exciting as it did forbidden, the burning stretch as his thumb slowly opened her, rubbing into the puckered entrance with a shallow, steady stroke that had her gasping and clutching for air.

Then he pulled his face slightly away from her, those dark, storm-flecked eyes looking up at her, and Denny's heart nearly stopped at the fierce, feral hunger she could see burning there, primitive and shadowed, dangerous and deadly. His mouth and chin glistened with her cream, lips parted as his breath rushed raggedly through his lungs. He just stared at her like that, as if trying to see into her soul, before lowering his eyes again—and Denny felt everything in her lower body spasm, a thick spill of cream slipping from her vulva as he gazed into the gasping need of her pussy.

Gabriel's lips parted, curled, and for the first time ever, she watched a wicked, boyish smile twist across that beautiful, scarred mouth. "Feel good, Denny?" he asked. At the same time, he pressed his other thumb down on her clit, pressing and rolling in a firm circular motion, and the friction—but more *that smile*—ripped her second orgasm out of her with such force, she didn't know how Jonah managed to keep her shuddering body in his arms. She shattered, body and soul, as the fiery pleasure rushed up through her in a fracturing pulse of hammering, violent bliss, pulling a series of keening, sexual cries from her throat that had never before known release. They'd been held deep inside, waiting for this moment of wrenching glory, ripped free by the sight of that gorgeous bad boy smile breaking across Gabriel Harrison's dangerous mouth.

"Oh Gabe, man, look at her," Jonah groaned into her shoulder. "She's like fire in my arms, shimmering and fucking beautiful."

Gabriel's eyes lifted, and she knew he was holding Jonah's blue-eyed gaze. His own gaze narrowed in silent communication, and then fell, catching again at her flushed face, his thumb still rubbing that teeth-grinding circle into her clit that was keeping the orgasm on such a writhing edge of ecstasy, it was almost more pain than pleasure. He blinked another slow, sensual shift of those long-lashed lids, and then his face pressed forward again, and that wickedly talented mouth closed over her drenched center, tongue lapping at her in avid strokes of need, as if he were desperate for the taste of the thick cream rushing from her womb. He pressed deeper, that rasping tongue digging deep inside her pussy, searching out the steady wash of juices slipping through the tight, rippling muscles, wicked thumbs on the pulse of her clit and her ass, and Denny cried out again, a harsh, frantic sound of gratification.

"That's it, Denny," Jonah grunted in her ear. "Come for him, sweet stuff. Come in his mouth and let him eat out all that sweet-smelling pussy juice that's driving me outta my mind." His head lowered, and he scratched his teeth over the sensitive stretch of muscle between her neck and shoulder, grinding the pounding length of his cloth-covered cock into her spine. "I love watching you get eaten out, sweet stuff. It's so fucking sexy. Give him all of it, Denny. Show him how much you want to be here."

And she did. She came all over him, arching and softly cursing, tears streaming from her eyes at the force of her release, a shivering burn flickering beneath the sensitive surface of her naked skin, making her tremble and moan. She licked her lips as she looked down at the man torturing her with pleasure, and that animal sound rumbled in his throat again, so sexy and hungry. Feral and impatient. Possessive and passion-filled. With a final, lingering, savoring lick, he lapped his warm tongue through her tingling folds, and pulled back, the silver flecks in those eyes glittering, the slate gray of his gaze still burning hot and fierce with hunger.

Holding her heavy-lidded stare, he carefully pulled his thumb from her ass, leaned back against the warm caramel leather of the couch, reached down with one hand, and began slowly flicking the buttons of his jeans. And, God help her, he was naked underneath. Denny nearly swallowed her tongue as one by one those buttons opened, the dark part in the fabric revealing first the silky black curls, and then her throat went dry at the first look at his brutal, beautiful cock. It was dark, ruddy and violently purple at the head, impossibly longer...thicker than she'd thought a man could be. And so damn powerful it made her womb convulse in hunger just to look at it.

"*Ohmygod*," she whispered, wetting her lips, eyes glued onto that massive cock, shocked and aroused and unbearably eager. What would it be like to taste? To feel that power throbbing between her lips, ripe with life and lust? To feel his cum pulsing down her throat while he shuddered and groaned with pleasure?

"Last chance, Denny," he muttered, the guttural snarl of his voice touching her deep inside, sparking another burning flash of arousal, even as the exhausting storm of ecstasy she'd just survived made its final, shivering withdrawal, a warm, heavy feeling left in its wake. "You ready to cry uncle, angel?"

"No. Never," she croaked, almost smiling at the odd sound of her voice after shouting out her pleasure.

He fisted one large hand around the wide root, squeezing hard as he stroked the thick, heavily veined stalk of dark, mouthwatering cock. "Don't forget you asked for it, Denny."

Damn right I did, she thought with a wonderful surge of pride, still amazed that she'd somehow found the courage to go through with this.

"Yeah, and she'll probably ask for a hell of a lot more," Jonah barked in a strained voice. "Stop trying to scare her off, you ass."

A strange look moved over Gabriel's face, something that lay in that mysterious chasm between violence and tenderness that could only be found in passion. Not just sex — not just screwing — but the raging kind of passionate, grinding, mind-shattering connection that could explode when it was a fuck that mattered. When it mattered more than anything in the world, who you accepted into your body and who you entered.

Denny had read about it, but never...*never* had she seen it with her own eyes, and the sight of it took her breath away.

"I'm not trying to scare her off," he grunted. "I just want to make sure that she understands exactly what she's getting herself into. No way in hell am I going to be able to hold back tonight. Do you understand that, Denny? Do you understand what that means?"

She knew he was warning her again, of something important, but she couldn't grasp onto a thought long enough to figure it out. Was simply unable to reason it through with that wicked erection making her body ache with a powerful, consuming craving. All she could do was nod her head, nearly drunk on the beauty of his body. "I understand that I want you," she moaned, not recognizing her voice. "I understand that I want you to stop talking and put your...your cock in my mouth. Let me taste it." She held his smoldering gray stare, knowing her emotions were washing over her flushed face, swimming through her eyes. "Let me make you feel good, Gabriel."

He didn't give her a response, but a tremble quaked through his powerful body, his fist knotting tighter around the broad root of his cock, its dark, ruddy skin flushed to a deep, bruised mark of color, and she knew her words had affected him. She kept her eyes on his as Jonah carefully lowered her legs, steadying her with his hands at her hips, when she would have simply melted to the floor, her legs were so rubbery. Then she licked her lips, needing to feel that magnificent hard-on in her mouth. Needing it *now*. "Gabriel..."

"Yeah?"

"I wouldn't be here if I didn't want this—didn't want *you*." Her smile was warm and womanly, sweetly inviting, meant to be a sensual, evocative assault on his senses, though she wasn't sure she could really pull off a smile like that. But she must have hit pretty close to the mark, because his narrowed eyes flashed with a wild, turbulent emotion too primitive to name, the muscles of his face going as taut as the straining tendons in that powerful neck.

"Hold her steady," he rumbled at Jonah, before reaching up and snagging the front of her bra, pulling her over until she bent at the waist, her ass shoved against Jonah and Gabriel's cock shoved right in her face.

"Open up, angel," Gabriel murmured in that throaty voice that she loved, the provocative scrape of sound binding her body in invisible chains of violent, volcanic need. In that moment, she felt as if she could consume him. Take him in through every hole and pore. His thumb found the corner of her swollen lips, pressing against the sensitive pad in a stroking, tempting caress, those gray eyes drawing her in deeper and deeper, until she felt she could reach inside of him and grab that burning ball of raw desire he kept struggling to control, hold it within the fragile cradle of her fingers, and melt the ice that imprisoned it, setting all that raging passion free.

He shifted, and his cock nudged her bottom lip, the molten silk of his cock head like the sweetest of sins. Denny was starved for it, her blood pulsing in a thundering rhythm, urging her to take. To lave and stroke, suckle and taste.

With one big fist clenched around the stunningly thick width of the heavy shaft, he nudged the column of flesh and blood against her mouth, stroking her lower lip in a carnal caress that was so wicked, she wanted to grin with naughty delight. Would have, but for the fact that if she didn't get him inside of her at the soonest possible moment, there was every chance she'd lose her mind.

Needing to know what that mouthwatering, throbbing, blatantly commanding cock tasted like, Denny flicked her tongue against the broad, wet tip, and nearly died as the pleasure burst over her taste buds.

"Mmm," she growled, pulling another shudder from him as the sound vibrated against his head. God, he tasted incredible. Addictive and hot and she wanted to taste it all.

With his eyes narrowed to sharp, piercing slits and hers heavy with lust and longing, she watched Gabriel rub the wet head of his dick against her lips, until her cranberry gloss was sticking to his skin, shiny and slick. He covered every inch of the delicate, slippery surfaces, bathed by her panting breaths, before finally nudging the thick, fat head of his cock just inside their inner rim, teasing her hunger as Jonah pulled her bare ass to his groin and groaned. With slow, deliberate strokes, Jonah rubbed his pants-covered cock against her soaking cleft, and Denny knew the drenched heat from her pussy had to be burning him through the front of his pants, just as Gabriel's cock scorched her lips.

God, she needed *more.*

More.

And as if he'd read her mind, Gabriel pressed the heavy head fully between her lips, inside of her mouth, those gray eyes glittering when she had to stretch as wide as she could to accommodate him.

"Damn, Denny. That's such a beautiful sight, angel," he rasped, voice ragged, stroking that stretched edge of her mouth with the trembling tip of one large, blunt finger. "Seeing those sexy sweet lips stretched around my dick—that hungry, animal look in your eyes—makes me fucking crazy. And you are hungry, aren't you, Denny?"

Her head bobbed in answer, that thick, throbbing flesh plunging an inch deeper, the slick drops of pre-cum slipping across her tongue, making her crave more. Making her crave as much as he could possibly give her. She tried to tell him with her eyes, with the hungry, avid stroke of her tongue around the thick, flared rim of his head, loving the taste and feel of him…the heat…the power.

He jolted, staring down at her, the savage look in his eyes saying that he wanted to throw her to the floor and screw her ever-loving brains out, while Jonah's hands clenched around her hips, his slacks-covered cock stroking a steady, powerful rhythm against her bare pussy that nearly had her eyes rolling back in her head.

"Show me, Denny." Gabriel stared at her, his face dark, lips wet and parted as his breath rushed raggedly from his wide chest. "Now, Denny. Show me if you're as good at sucking cock as I've always dreamed you'd be." He muttered the words past those sexy, carnal lips, the dazed pleasure in his smoldering gaze making her wonder if he even knew what he was saying. But it didn't matter. She was beyond ready to show him how *good* she could be. Ready to prove how badly she needed the feel of him driving into her mouth, hard and deep, exploding into her throat.

He smelled like fine Scotch and sin, male animal and master, but his cock, God, his cock tasted like sin-pleasured heaven. Hot, musky, a little salty, the power throbbing within the tight stretch of her lips acted like the most powerful aphrodisiac on her senses. It drugged her with the pleasure, drumming against the sensitive pad of her tongue, pulsing within the bruising stretch of her lips, and Denny found herself suddenly sucking with a skill she'd never known she possessed.

"Oh hell. That's it, angel," he grated, jaw hard and eyes wild, his body held tight, every long, strong muscle rigid with tension. His big hands tangled in her hair, long fingers pressing into her scalp, and his hips jerked, forcing more of his thick flesh into her mouth—yet, still somehow careful enough not to give her too much. "That's so fucking good. Suck my cock, Denny. Suck on it, angel. Show me how much you like having this pretty little mouth stuffed full of dick."

And she did. She went wild on him, greedy and hungry for the brutally hard, impossibly thick flesh in her mouth, wishing she could take all of it. Her earlier attempts at giving head had always been awkward, frustrating, and too much thought. Now she realized she'd never really been into it enough to lose herself to the lust and the need. With Gabriel, there was no thought, only primitive hunger and instinct as she worshipped him with the sliding clasp and suction of her lips, her mouth and tongue eager tools of pleasure.

"Shit, Gabe, she's on fire. I want inside," Jonah grunted behind her, his deep voice thick with impatience as his hips repeatedly rubbed the hard ridge of his cock against her cleft, his strong fingers biting into her hips the only thing keeping her on her feet.

Gabriel made some kind of indistinct snarl in answer, and Jonah laughed, a deep, rich sound that was wicked as hell. "What's the matter, Gabe?" he drawled, though his voice was tight with arousal. "Is she pushing you, man? Ripping that legendary control of yours right out from under you?"

Through her lashes, Denny watched as Gabriel sent a hot, furious glare over her head, his fingers pressing harder against her scalp, like he meant to keep her from pulling away, and she wondered if he even realized that he'd done it.

"You think you're so damn smart, don't you, Jonah?"

Jonah snorted. "Not fucking hardly," he laughed, but it was rough with hunger. "If I was smart, buddy, it'd be my dick in heaven right now, instead of yours."

Gabriel grunted, and Jonah leaned over her back, looking over her shoulder to watch her sucking on his best friend's cock. "Damn, Denny," he muttered. "That looks fucking amazing, sweet stuff."

"Feels even better," Gabriel gritted with a hard smile.

"Yeah," Jonah drawled dryly, leaning back to place a wet kiss at her nape, and the innocent caress sent chills racing across her skin, making him chuckle. "I can just imagine how good it feels, you lucky bastard."

Denny smiled around the head of Gabriel's cock, and took a deep breath through her nose. His sexy, masculine scent flooded through her, and she worked harder to get the top part of that huge erection between her lips, their fleshy surfaces feeling swollen and stretched by his brutal size. Her hands moved from where she'd gripped onto the hard muscles of his thighs, to brace against the soft sofa on either side of his hips, nails pricking the fine leather, as she struggled to keep her balance against Jonah's thrusting, exciting strokes against the wet, enflamed cushion of her pussy.

As if he sensed her need, Gabriel twisted his fists into the wild tangle of her hair, gripping the sides of her head in a hard, controlling hold that had her pussy gushing again, her thick juices slipping from her folds as he worked her over him. That primitive, controlling look in his gray gaze demanded she hold his stare while he watched the top inches of his dick move in and out of her mouth, deeper and deeper, her tongue lashing his hot skin and her cheeks sucking in as she tried to feed off of him, eager for his taste and pleasure.

And then she felt Jonah's movements slow as his hands began moving over her body, leaving her hips to skim down her thighs, trailing up her abdomen to roll her nipples between his fingers before reaching back and gripping her ass. He kneaded the flesh of her cheeks with an appreciative growl, and then stroked one finger across that tender, puckered hole—and Denny felt a strange little click inside of her head, as if a door had been unlocked, and something that was almost frightening crept through. Something primal and untamed, primordial and ancient, as if her inner wild woman had finally been released...and she was hungry. Ravenous. Ready to be laid out and taken, penetrated and claimed in every possible way that they could physically take her.

His fingers slipped lower, teasing the sensitive, puffy lips of her pussy while Gabriel's cock steadily surged into her, and she cried out around the thick flesh shafting her mouth, as savage and desperate to give pleasure as she was to receive it. It should have frightened her, the ferocity of these feelings, but she was lost in it—a pure being of need and passion.

"Damn, you feel so good, Denny," Jonah muttered at her back, dipping his thumb into her pussy. He thrust it there for a moment, swirling in her juices, and then pulled it out and brushed that wet thumb against her tiny asshole, slowly pushing it inside of that tight, puckered ring of muscle, stretching her open, gently working it into her, until the entire blunt digit was buried up her ass, sending that strange pleasure/pain coursing through her blood again. She moaned around Gabriel's cock, and Jonah curled his fingers forward, sending two deep into her pussy. She squirmed from the dual penetration, and he began working her on his hand while the other reached back around her chest to find a tight, aching nipple. He twisted and milked the puckered tip, and she groaned, shouting around Gabriel's cock, lashing his hot shaft with her tongue.

"Hot and tight, and so fucking wet," Jonah growled, working her harder, his fingers and thumb moving in tandem, finger-fucking her while Gabe began thrusting into her mouth, careful not to give her too much, but still pushing to the back of her throat.

"I can't wait to get my dick in you, sweet stuff. Can't wait to find out what it feels like, sinking into Denny Abbott's hot little cunt." Jonah curved himself over her, putting his mouth at her ear, his words a dark promise of intent that had her vising around his fingers, while the added bite of Gabriel's hands fisted in her hair, tugging gently as he shafted into her mouth faster and faster, nearly made her scream. "I can't wait to be where Gabe is, sweetheart. Can't wait 'til it's my cock drilling your pretty little mouth, shooting my cum down your throat."

"Shut up, Jonah," Gabriel snarled, and his lips pulled back over his teeth as she relaxed her throat and took him a bit deeper, desperate to do exactly as she'd promised and make him feel good. Wonderfully, impossibly, breathtakingly good.

Pleasure rushed in on her, heavy and fast, the wicked feel of Jonah's clever fingers and thumb and Gabriel's delicious cock pulsing against the tender pad of her tongue, making her feel as if she were lost in the violent, lashing winds of a carnal storm. The ecstasy of it ripped through her, powerful and demanding, and she found herself sucking at his thrusting cock as savagely as Jonah pumped his thumb up her ass, his fingers dipping deeper and deeper into her melting pussy.

Oh god. She wanted...*had to* feel Gabriel exploding into her mouth when Jonah made her come. Had to feel his cum jetting down her throat—knowing she was the woman to pull the heat from this man who only ever shared the ice.

His long fingers tightened in her hair, warning her, but she sucked harder, filled with heat and hunger, refusing to pull away, stubbornly demanding the loss of that infuriating control.

"Denny," he growled, bucking against her, the scent of his skin growing stronger, hot and sweaty and utterly male, just as Jonah forced her over the edge again and pleasure exploded through her, vibrating within every cell. "If you don't want my cum pumping down your throat, pull back, angel. Fuck, I'm gonna come. *Now, Denny,*" he roared in a rough, guttural shout as she sobbed around his rigid flesh. "*Right now.*"

Gabriel watched Denny's gaze burn up at him, all burnished warmth, acceptance, and passion, and the orgasm pulled up from his balls in a thundering explosion that turned him inside out. It left him reeling, shaking and pumping into that sweet little hole of her mouth while his muscles seized and his back arched, his cum shooting painfully from the head of his dick in powerful spurts that he knew must be choking her. But she only sucked him harder, with the most delicious suction he'd ever experienced, stroking him with her greedy little tongue, demanding every sizzling drop, until she'd drained him.

A deep, hoarse groan rumbled from his chest, and as he surfaced from that dazed fog of lust-filled satisfaction, he realized he'd just fucked himself to heaven between those luscious lips. Fucked Denny Abbott's beautiful little face while she gave him the most mind-blowing, sweetest fucking head he'd ever had.

God help him, it'd been the most amazing experience of his life.

And yet, the look in her eyes threw him. Shit, who was he kidding? It scared the hell out of him, and he retreated in the only way that he could, untangling his hands from her hair and then drawing back his hips as he gently, with shaking fingers, pushed her face away, and pulled his cock, still thick with blood and lust, from her swollen lips. She made a soft, throaty sigh at his withdrawal, and Gabriel knew that she could sense him on a deeper level—one that required no words—and it made his gut go tight with tension.

He leaned his head against the back of the sofa, allowed his eyes to drift close, and ripped one trembling hand through his short hair. With slow, deep breaths, he tried to regain control as the seconds ticked by and his heart continued to pound a violent rhythm within his chest. He felt barbaric in his need for possession, but knew he needed to distance himself and regroup, before taking the next step.

And there was no doubt that he'd take it—and many more, before this night was over. Damn it, he had to get his fill of her. Had to saturate himself in her heat and sweetness until there was enough to get him through—get him by—tomorrow and the next day, day by day.

And then the sound of a soft, sweet sigh, accompanied by wet, suctioning noises and Jonah's feral groans ripped him back to the moment. He lifted his heavy lids, and the sight that met his eyes was one that at any other time would have had him seeing red, but not tonight. Tonight, within this warm, wood-scented room—that heavier fragrance accented by the crisp, delectable scent of Denny's ripe, succulent pussy and cum—was something beyond comprehension. They'd entered a new consciousness here, breathing within some foreign, alternate reality where the rule of the day was pleasure, both that given and received…and even witnessed.

Gabriel leaned forward, planting his elbows on his spread knees, his cock still wet and throbbing even harder than before, to the point where he marveled that there was even enough blood left in his brain for thought.

But he was thinking. There was no doubt about that. Thinking about every raunchy, nasty, mind-shattering act he planned on acting out upon her gorgeous little ass tonight. His fingers made quick work of the buttons down the front of his shirt, and he pulled it from his arms as he gained his feet, ignoring the screaming in his knee, eyes burning hot with hunger as he moved closer. With his jeans hanging loose on his hips, he stood at her hip, looking down at where Jonah had placed her upon the plush backdrop of his favorite rug, an Oriental masterpiece of deep blues, greens, and creams. Gabriel blinked slowly, feeling the rush of lust through his hunger-thickened system, a heady flow of sexual craving, gain a thundering momentum in his pulse.

He gazed down with a wicked, carnal smile, watching Jonah shove his face between those widespread thighs, his tongue shoved so far up her addictive little cunt, Gabe wondered if he was actually stroking her G-spot. From the flushed look of pleasure washing over Denny's face, her beautiful eyes squeezed tightly shut, teeth biting into that plump lower lip, he wouldn't be surprised.

And Jonah was lost in her—completely caught up in the lush scents and tastes of her soft, female body. It was amazing to watch as the hungers pulled him from point to point, all the enticing dips and swells, hollows and planes that lured a man to want to sip and devour, tasting her from head to toe. Jonah's mouth alternately suckled at her now naked tits and her bare, cream-covered pussy lips, eating at her juices as if he couldn't get enough of her. Her shoes and bra had obviously been removed, along with Jonah's sweater, while he'd been regrouping, and the sight of those delicate, swollen nipples atop the fine, translucent skin of her quivering breasts had

Gabriel's tongue stroking the roof of his mouth, eager for his own chance to taste and devour, suckle and stroke.

"Christ," Jonah groaned, rasping voice muffled by the swollen, drenched lips of her cunt. "Denny, you taste so damn good, sweet stuff."

"Beautiful," Gabriel rumbled, and no sooner had the hoarsely spoken word left his mouth, than her eyes shot open, the warm brown luminous with desire, swirling in a tumble of rich amber and sable. Her neck arched, arms flung wide, that rosy, just-fucked mouth opened on a silent cry, as the heat from his gaze seemed to burn across her skin in a wildfire of lust-fueled need.

"Jonah was right, Denny. It's a beautiful sight, watching your sexy little cunt get eaten out, the satisfaction and hunger washing over you until you glow." His fist tightened, knuckles turning white as he reached down and pumped his cock until he wondered if he'd actually spill into the air, showering over her in hard, violent expulsions of cum. Grinding his jaw, feeling his damn knees tremble, Gabriel squeezed down, hard, and held it back. Held it in, because the next time he shot his load, he wanted it to be deep inside the biting clench of that hot, tender pussy. Wanted to feel those exquisite, fist-tight little muscles sucking on his dick, trying to swallow him whole, while he fucked her apart, cramming himself in to the hilt, forcing those narrow walls to take the brutal width and length of his cock.

He wanted to shaft her with every aching, pounding inch, more than he wanted to breathe. To live to see another day. More than he'd ever wanted anything...or anyone, in his entire godforsaken life.

"Christ, she's incredible," he grunted, the words gritted through his teeth as he struggled to hold himself together and not blurt out everything breaking open inside of him.

"As ripe for sucking as they come," Jonah moaned, playing now with one puckered, blushing nipple between his lips, pulling and tugging at the sensitive flesh. "There isn't a flat spot on her, Gabe. These curves of hers are sexy as hell. And she tastes like sin. Hell, I feel like I could get drunk on her, it's so damn good."

"Just don't enjoy it too much," he muttered, wondering where his sudden caveman routine was coming from. Hell, when they were younger, before he'd met Karen, and when he was still stupid enough to believe that life was going to work out just the way he wanted it to, he'd never balked at sharing a woman with his best friend.

But then it'd *never* been like this. *Never.*

Those women had not been *Denny*—and that right there made all the difference.

"Is there such a thing as enjoying her too much?" That taunting, teasing grin played over Jonah's mouth again, his tongue licking at his lower lip, catching more of her glistening juice, making Gabe long to wipe it away with his fist.

When you're eating my woman, there is, but he choked back the surprising words of possession, unwilling to make such a telling admission—confession. Because one thing was beginning to become crystal fucking clear here, like the pure blue waters of a frigid mountain lake.

Jonah was on to him.

The bastard was testing him, and goddamn it, he was going to prove to the ass that he wasn't going to fall head over heels for this woman. Want her—yes. Want to fuck her raw and keep his cock buried in her as deep as he could get it for as long as humanly possible—hell yes. But care for her? No—no way in hell. He'd been there, at that place before, and he'd sucked at it. He was too reckless, too rough, too violent to keep something so fragile and pure without wrecking it. He'd done it once, and the pain still ate at him. He wouldn't let himself make the same mistake again.

And if the little voice in the back of his head was laughing its ass off, knowing he was lying through his teeth, Gabriel chose to ignore it. Ignored it for the sheer friggin' fact that he needed *this*. Needed what was being offered here tonight—and was helpless to resist. Needed to get his mouth into her cunt again and eat his way to heaven before he starved from the gut-clawing want he'd been carrying around since hiring her luscious ass.

Christ, he'd never experienced anything like it. Never—and that was almost the worst of all. Karen had been in love with him, and if he wasn't such a bastard, maybe he'd have been able to love her in return—but he hadn't. Whatever feelings he'd held for her had paled in comparison to the mere sight and sound of Denny Abbott. What kind of an ass did that make him? Karen was dead because of him, and here he'd gone and given what she'd wanted to this woman who was little more than a stranger.

Yeah, "this woman"—as if someone as remarkable as Denny could be catalogued as a mere "anything"—who could have him dragging his tongue around after her if she wanted. Who could make or break him with so little effort.

And now it was so much fucking worse. Now there was no going back. He had her creamy little cunt spread open for his eyes, her warm, female smell, like melted sugar and honey, filling his nose, his tongue stroking the roof of his mouth, eager to dip inside of her and root out more of that lust-flavored cum. It was syrupy sweet, making his head spin as if he'd been on a bender.

Jonah tipped his face up again from between her legs, his mouth glistening with her cream, tongue slipping past his bottom lip to lick at the decadent juices covering his skin. Gabriel's eyes narrowed, the sensual heat banked for but a moment, as he stared at the obvious enjoyment Jonah took in her taste.

Feeling fierce and possessive, aching with lust from the soles of his feet up to the top of his head, he stared down at his best friend and the woman he lo—*No!*—the woman he *wanted*. The woman he *wanted* to screw through the floor and the wall and his bed. Anywhere. Everywhere. He wanted to fuck her beautiful little brains out in every possible way there was. Hell, at this point, he might even make up a few.

"She'd better tell me now if there's anything she won't do—anything she won't have done to her."

Her eyes widened, a tiny spark of fear and excitement flickering through her gaze at his question.

"She'll do whatever you want, won't you, Denny?" Jonah drawled with a slow, boyish smile.

Gabriel's mouth tightened, fist biting into the thick root of his cock. "I need to hear her say it."

"Tell him, Denny," Jonah crooned softly, stroking the tender folds of her pussy, as if he were reassuring her with his touch. "Give him what he needs, sweet stuff."

"Anything," she rasped, the lust-thickened voice sounding so unlike her, she blinked up at him in shock at the hungry sound. But the flare of heat that burned in his smoldering gaze seemed to give her the strength to say it all. "Whatever you want, Gabriel. *Anything.*"

He jerked his head toward her lush body laid out on the carpet, the rough words once again gritted through his teeth as he fought for control. "I get first fuck of all these perfect, pink little holes, Denny. And then—"

"Then what, Gabe?" Jonah challenged, looking as if he'd explode if he sent him home right then. And the truth of the matter was that he couldn't do this without Jonah. He needed the balance, or he'd be lost. It was too dangerous, because if he wasn't careful, he'd find himself tying her up to his bed with the intention of never letting her go. Talking rings on their fingers and the whole friggin' nine yards.

Uh-uh. No way. Can't risk it.

Hardening his jaw, Gabriel ignored the taunting glint in Jonah's deep blue gaze. "Then I'll watch him fuck you, Denny. Watch it and enjoy it, but I get you first. Everything, Denny. All of you. Ever been taken in that pretty little ass, angel?"

She shook her head rapidly from side to side, those warm brown eyes widening with surprise…and unmistakable excitement. It worried her, and yet, she wanted it. He could see the want slithering beneath her skin, rippling with anticipation.

"Yeah, I wouldn't have thought so. Your cunt's so damn tight, I don't think you've fucked much there either. But we're going to change all that, Denny. Here and now, it's all going to change. And once I start—I won't stop."

Not ever, his heart snarled, giving him a moment's pause before his lust beat back the trepidation and uncertainty, shuttling him headfirst into the hungry demands of his flesh and blood. "But you have to be sure it's what you want."

She blinked slowly up at him, the flickering firelight kissing her tender female flesh. "Do you…" she whispered, her voice softly hesitant for the first time that night. "Do you really want *me*?"

"Yeah." One word, so full of meanings, some he didn't even understand—couldn't explain, identify or catalog within the raging chaos of his sanity at that moment, when hunger struggled for dominance and control.

Her chin rose, that angelic face etched with bone-deep determination, damn near bringing him to his knees then and there. "Then, I want this, Gabriel. All of it. *Everything*."

Chapter Six

❧

She wanted it. All of it. *Everything.*

Denny meant every word — and from the look of things, Gabriel Harrison was more than ready to give her whatever she asked for.

She'd opened her eyes, surfacing on the river of pleasure Jonah continued to skillfully sweep her along, to see Gabriel standing over her, stroking his cock, watching her with those gripping gray eyes. The seconds seemed like hours, her gaze flickering between that spellbinding stare and mouthwatering cock, unable to decide where it should settle. The glimmering fluid leaking from the slit in the heavy head had tasted hot and salty-sweet against her tongue, making her crave more, and now her tongue stroked her lower lip as she burned in memory — but the look in those stormy eyes ripped at her. So many emotions swirled there in the wild, silvery depths, like a raging wintry sea, bringing her under his spell. Set that tiny flame of a dream that Jonah had kindled earlier with his outrageous beliefs of how Gabriel felt about her to a flickering blaze of full-blown hope.

"Gabe will give over his heart, because once he gets his dick in you," Jonah had whispered roughly in her ear, his strong hands gently tying the silk off at the back of her head, "once he buries himself up your sweet cunt and feels you come apart around him, he'll know that he can't fight it any longer."

Yes, those remembered words gave her hope. Desperate, longing hope that made her want to pound upon that broad, masculine chest and demand he open his heart. But she couldn't do that. All she could do was give of herself. To make demands would send Gabriel running so fast her head would spin.

But she held on to the hope like a wish that could be hers, if she could only reach up and grab the falling star, capturing its fire within the palm of her hand. She'd been under his spell from the moment she had first set eyes on him. From that first interview, when he'd met her in the hallway outside his office and invited her in, taking his seat behind his imposing desk, wearing a dark suit, dark tie, and equally dark expression, questioning her in that deep, dark voice.

He'd been so utterly imposing, the starched silk of his crisp, white shirt gleaming in perfect contrast against the dark, golden tan of his skin, dark hand rolling a gold pen through his long fingers as he'd leaned back in his leather chair and studied her with the acute perception of a hawk going in for the kill. A part of her — one that fed on fear and intuition — had wanted to run, to flee before she lost some part of herself in that cold, mesmerizing gray gaze. And yet, she hadn't moved.

Instead, she'd fallen, headfirst and without a safety net, into that frightening emotional landscape.

And what had pulled her in was the way he'd held his other hand against the lower part of his face and rubbed his fingers across his lips, as if it were a casual gesture, when her heart suspected he was just trying to hide his scar from her watchful eyes, embarrassed by the imperfection. Considering what she knew now, maybe even ashamed of what it represented. But that one inherently innocent, utterly human action had given her the first glimpse into the "real" man who lived hidden beneath that cold armor of control. Had nestled itself into the until then empty part of her where everlasting, untainted and pure love could grow — blossoming from that fledgling seed into an awesome, undeniable matter of the heart that had slowly, day by day, invaded her soul.

What do you want, Gabriel? Could you truly want...me?

Or...was it just the thrill of a ménage that was getting him off tonight? Was she only seeing what she wanted to see in those gorgeous, long-lashed, turbulent eyes? Inventing excuses for why it was the "right" thing to do—her being there—his best friend stroking his wicked tongue up the tiny opening of her pussy with delicious skill, her juices flowing smooth and free as he ate her out, while Gabriel looked on with that naked hunger darkening his silver gaze, big fist knotted around his cock, long fingers barely able to close around it. He *was* that thick, so much so that she'd had to work hard to stretch her mouth around him. He'd been patient, feeding himself into her bit by bit, until she'd been able to take the top portion, his fist working the bottom half of his thick root until he'd tangled them both in her hair—but what would it be like when he fed that massive erection into her *gone-too-long-without-a-man* pussy? Would he be as patient—or would he force it in with a hard, heavy, unforgiving thrust that crammed him in to the hilt?

She shivered with the thought, her inner muscles clenching in need, and Jonah groaned into her as she clamped down on his tongue, the rough sound vibrating through her tender tissues, pulling another throaty cry from her lips.

"Make her come again, Jonah. Make her come down your throat while I watch."

The words emerged rough and guttural, growled from that wicked mouth that Gabriel no longer shielded from her, and the jagged scrape of erotic sound sent Denny into another shivering spasm of delight. It was as if she could feel them rolling over the sensitive, dewy folds of her pulsing flesh, nestling within her vagina like the slow, torturous thrusting of Jonah's strong, wicked tongue.

"Do you hear that, Denny?" Jonah drawled, dragging the flat of his tongue across her juicy slit, and she knew she was flooding against him, drenching him with her cream. "Gabe wants you to come in my mouth, sweet stuff. *I* want you to come in my mouth." He trailed his tongue up the swollen pads of her lips, dipping and exploring, leaving no part of her untouched...untasted. "Don't think I could ever get enough of this delicious little cunt. It's like honey and sugar, sweetheart. Makes me want to lick you up like a treat, head buried between these beautiful thighs, my face shoved in this pretty pussy twenty-four hours a day."

"Don't go too far, Jonah," Gabriel warned from above.

"Too far?" Jonah snorted, his breath warm against her tender flesh while he teased her clit with his nose, gently tickling the tip of his tongue around her vulva. "No such thing with Denny, Gabe. This isn't my dirty little club and I'm not putting on a show for you, man. I'm just speaking the truth. She's fucking addictive."

"But she doesn't belong to you, does she?" Gabriel's voice was soft, and sounded all the more dangerous for it.

Denny took a deep breath, wondering just how far Jonah planned on pushing him. "I don't *belong* to either of you," she said, wetting her lips. *But I want to. God, how I want to.*

Jonah lifted his auburn head, staring at her over the panting rise of her breasts, her nipples still tight and wet from his mouth. "Damn, you hear that, Gabe? You gonna let her get away with it?" he teased. "Maybe we need to try harder to convince her." His handsome face lowered, and his tongue dipped back into her quivering pussy, thrusting inside of her with such decadent skill, she couldn't hold back a raw, husky cry.

"You...you two have done this before," she panted, twisting beneath the hungry mastery of Jonah's mouth, "haven't you?"

Gabriel stared down at her, his eyes no longer cold, but roiling with heat as he watched her writhe in pleasure, his sharp cheekbones dark with color. "Not since we were old enough to know better."

"Why does that not surprise me?" she gasped, knowing, instinctively, that they hadn't shared a woman since Gabriel's girlfriend had died.

Jonah licked his way back up to her thrumming clit, his hair tickling her skin as it brushed against her thighs. "Do you want to be surprised, sweet stuff?" he moaned. "I can give you surprises. Shock the sex juices right out of you, if that's the way you want it." To prove his point, he caught her ripe clit gently in his teeth and tugged, ripping a husky shout up from her heaving chest, her pussy clenching, desperate for something hard and thick to fill it, packing her full.

She opened her mouth and tried to respond, that impetuous wild woman inside of her ready to beg someone to fuck her, damn it, when Jonah moved to his knees between her shamelessly spread legs and said, "Touch yourself, Denny. Touch your pretty little pussy and show Gabe those flushed inner lips, all cherry red and sweet, hidden inside. Let him see how hot and wet we make you. How on fire you are."

She trembled, feeling even more exposed than before, but her fingers were already settling on her tummy. They moved in a slow, teasing caress over her skin, inching down toward her splayed sex with every intention of following his lead. Of showing them how she masturbated in her bed at night, her fingers slipping through her warm juices, fingering her pussy until she brought at least a flash of relief, if not a mind-blowing orgasm.

"Oh Christ," Gabriel growled, and Denny looked up to find him fisting both hands around his powerful, heavy cock, the fat, purple head soaked now with the glistening streams of pre-cum, looking like it would explode. His shoulders bunched with power, arms long and hard with sinew, skin gleaming with sweat, and she knew she'd never seen a more erotic sight than him standing there above her. "This'll fucking kill me."

Her lips curled in a slow, womanly smile at his snarled words, and she felt a flare of power...of feminine confidence burn through her that she'd never before experienced. It was a white-hot, blinding rush of sensation, one she could so easily get addicted to, knowing she'd made him like this. Knowing that he wanted to fuck her so badly she could all but feel the waves of lust and carnal appetite pulsing off of his tall, hard, dangerous body.

She kept her eyes on his, feeding off of the red, pulsing glow of his sharp-edged hunger, and let her own hunger take her over. Her fingers slipped across the slippery, swollen wetness of her pussy, and she used her left hand to spread her outer lips, opening the deeply pink inner flesh to Gabriel's smoldering stare. And he was staring. Those beautiful gray eyes were glued onto the provocative sight of her open sex, nearly making her come from his look alone.

And she couldn't forget Jonah. His big hands bit into the tender flesh on the backs of her knees, pulling them out high and wide, giving the muscles of her pussy that extra stretch that felt like a wicked, sin-drenched heaven. Dark red, silky strands of his hair fell over his high brow, that glittering blue stare joining Gabriel's gray one, and together they watched, captivated, as she fluttered the fingers of her right hand over the exposed inner folds of her sex. She teased, twirling them over and around the puffy rim of her vulva, her juices making her fingers slick as she trailed them back up to the hardened bud of her clit. Then she pressed the outer lips harder, wider, knowing her clit was swollen and crimson, throbbing there at the top of her open…*cunt*, and she began to rub.

Her back arched, lids fluttering as she tried to keep the wild, savage expressions on their faces in focus, while her index finger stroked rapidly over her clit, sending shockwaves of pleasure racing through her blood, tensing her muscles. A low moan broke from her throat, and she watched Gabriel work his jaw, could almost hear the harsh grinding of his teeth as his dark, blistering stare began moving back and forth between her masturbating fingers and the place where her teeth bit sharply into her lower lip, nearly drawing blood.

"Hell," Jonah growled. He flexed his fingers, forcing her legs up higher, tilting her hips. "You're so fucking sexy, I'm going to come in my goddamn pants, sweet stuff. Friggin' explode just from watching you."

A rough cry broke out of her throat, breasts rising with her rapid breaths, and she slipped her soaked fingers lower, plunging two slim digits into the tight depths of her pussy before dragging them back up to circle her aching clit, and then plunge them deep inside again.

"*Fuck*," Gabriel grated in a voice so low, she could barely make out what he said. Denny found herself plunging her fingers faster, wanting to watch him lose control, needing to push him over that infuriating edge.

"Not yet," Jonah grunted, demanding her attention, and her fingers slowed as she looked at him, the looming orgasm softly receding to swirl through the pulse of her blood, waiting until it would be granted release. Jonah trembled, the muscles of his mouthwatering body savagely hard as he knelt there between her widespread thighs, chest gleaming and eyes burning a violent, volcanic blue. The front of his slacks bulged with the huge bulk of his cock, and she couldn't help but blink in fascinated appreciation of his beauty.

"First," he grunted, "first, I want you to tell him what you think about when you lie in bed at night and play with this perfect, starving little cunt. Tell Gabe whose face you see when you slip these pretty fingers into your sweet pussy, Denny." He let go of one thigh and grasped onto her right wrist, pulling her hand to his face. A brief, hard smile flickered at the corners of his wide mouth, and then he parted his lips and licked his tongue against her index finger, lapping at the sticky essence of her cream, rumbling with pleasure. "Damn, that's delicious. Now tell him, sweet stuff."

"I...I can't," she argued achingly, looking up at Gabriel, her chest feeling tight, stomach knotted from the way he was watching her, like he couldn't decide whether he wanted to kiss her or put her over his knee and smack her backside.

"Are you too afraid to say his name?" Jonah taunted, nipping the pad of her thumb, then pulling the wet digit into his mouth and suckling.

"*N-n-no*," she stammered, ripping her eyes away from Gabriel to glare at the man tormenting her. "If he's too blind to figure it out, then he doesn't deserve to know."

Jonah shook his head and laughed, the golden light from the fire shimmering across the deep, dark red of his hair, the hard angles of his face. "Oh, he isn't blind, sweetheart. A stubborn bastard, yes, but he isn't blind.

"Come on," he whispered, placing a tender kiss to her palm, to the skittering pulse in her wrist. "Just admit it to him, Denny. Whose cock is it you think about pumping into you, cramming through those tight little walls, pumping your beautiful brains out? When you touch yourself with these slender fingers and pinch your nipples, biting your gorgeous lip, writhing in your bed, whose face do you see when you close your eyes and fall over the edge? Who do you imagine eating you out, shoving his face in your pink little cunt and licking you until you come down his throat? Who do you imagine pushing your legs up and wide, spreading you open, watching his cock pounding into you, ramming inside this snug little hole, making you scream?"

She twisted in his grip, flushed and suddenly furious at being cornered, but another mind-blowing orgasm was wailing through her system, brought on by his husky words, and she was helpless against the need to gain her release. "You already know who, damn it!" she choked out in a harsh rush of words, hating that her eyes were going wet with tears, wondering if she looked as foolish as she felt. "He already knows, Jonah!" Her voice rang out unusually loud in the quiet room, and she couldn't help but look back up at Gabriel, her breath catching in her throat at the effect of her words on him. He looked on the verge of violence, savage and primed for a fight, but she wasn't afraid of him. At least not in a physical sense.

No—it was on a purely emotional level that he utterly terrified her.

"Yeah, I think you might be right," Jonah laughed on a rough burst of air. "I think the lucky bastard knows *exactly* who he is, sweet stuff." And then, as if he were prodding a cornered animal with a stick, he said, "But maybe I should try harder to change your mind. Maybe if I blow your little sex circuits hard enough, you'll see my face when you close your eyes at night, Denny. Only, I won't make you settle for these beautiful hands of yours. I'm more than willing to hold you tight and fuck you. To give you everything." He lowered her hand and pressed her damp palm against the throbbing length of his pants-covered cock, the brutal thickness drumming against her flesh, jerking beneath her touch, desperate for its own release. "Maybe I'm ready to blow your mind and make you crave what *I* can give you."

Gabriel shifted closer, until his right foot actually touched her side. "Cut the crap, Jonah."

Jonah sent an innocent look up at the man towering over them. "Who said it's crap, Gabe? You don't think I've wanted her just as badly as you have?"

He released his clenched hands from around his massive cock, the heavy head so wet, it was nearly dripping, and fisted them at his sides. "She's not yours to want or take. You don't get that choice."

Licking her lips, Denny fought for her voice, her breath still shallow and fast. "I hate to interrupt the testosterone fest, but 'she' happens to be right here, and she's tired of being talked over like she doesn't exist."

Gabriel cut his glittering gray gaze back to her, and she gasped at the savagery of his look, so open and raw, everything right there for her to see. Then he closed his eyes, took two deep, sharp breaths, and when he looked back down at her, she could see him struggling to retreat behind that infuriating wall of ice. Too damn bad it wasn't working, she thought with a hopeful, glowing inner smile.

"Don't," he rasped, "for one second, Denny, think that I could ever miss the fact that you exist. I've taken in every breath that you drew, every smile that spread across that beautiful mouth, since you first marched that gorgeous ass of yours into my office. So don't, for one goddamn moment, think I'm not taking in every single thing about you. I've got every little intimate detail imprinted in my mind, and they sure as hell aren't going anywhere."

She held her breath, waiting to see if Jonah would push him with this sudden, amazing, heart-stopping confession, his words spreading through her like a fiery rush of pleasure—but Jonah only lowered his head and smiled against the moist cushion of her pussy, either enjoying himself too much to push anymore right then, or believing that now wasn't the time.

"I believe you said I should make her come in my mouth, right, Gabe?" he drawled, grinning, and then softly closed that devilish mouth over her throbbing clit.

A lazy smirk played at the corner of Gabriel's lips, and he nodded his dark head, never taking his eyes from hers as he took his cock back into the biting grip of his right hand, slowly stroking the rigid rod of flesh. "Yeah. That's what I want to see. Make her come, Jonah, right down your throat."

"My pleasure," the gorgeous redhead murmured, and then those rough-silk lips captured the tiny bud, working it so expertly—that primitive fire burning from up above in Gabriel's dark eyes—and everything went black inside her mind. Silent and heavy, like the quiet before the terrifying wreckage of the storm. She was already so on edge, the pleasure hit her hard and fast and sharp this time, exploding from her womb with a force so violent, it left her arching, writhing on the rug as the world disappeared and she lost herself in the rushing, thundering explosion.

"That's it," Gabriel grated, his lips pulling back over his teeth as he watched her, clenching his cock so fiercely that the veins on the back of his scarred hand stood out in savage relief. "That's it, Denny. Pump that sweet, hot little cunt into his face and make him eat your cum. Let him get his fill of it now, angel, because after tonight, he isn't ever getting it again."

Jonah growled in protest against Gabriel's statement, pressing his face deeper into her pussy, his tongue plunging deeper and deeper into her clenching sheath, and she could feel his throat working as he swallowed her juices. Everything, all of it, crashed down on her, and her mouth opened, shouts or cries ripping from her throat that she couldn't grasp, lost as she was beneath the crushing waves as they pummeled her, tossing her helplessly in the throes of sensations too sharp to be borne.

When she came back, her body lay soft and pliant, fingers curled innocently into her open palms, and Gabriel still stood there, a soft, almost gentle smile of amazement twisting across that scarred, carnal mouth—killing the embarrassment Denny had been so sure she would feel, coming beneath the mouth of another man, while the one she *loved* looked on. But he didn't make her feel dirty or immoral. That simple, wicked, kind of uneasy smile made her feel...special. Made her feel like she mattered, no matter how little, to this powerful man who let *no one* matter. Who allowed nothing and no one to touch him.

And yet, she did. His earlier words were proof of that, and Denny could see it there in that boyish grin, and it made her want to smile in return, if only her muscles would follow the most simple of commands. But she was too limp with pleasure. It pumped heavily through her veins, like a narcotic, making her greedy flesh burn with the need for more. A need she knew he could see, it blazed so brightly.

Slowly, he turned his head and cut an intense look down at Jonah, one black brow arched in inquiry. "I don't suppose you thought to bring rubbers?"

"Fuck, I brought the beautiful woman," Jonah laughed from where he'd collapsed against the giving cushion of her thigh, the auburn silk at his temples damp against his face as he struggled for breath. "Do I have to do everything?"

"I'll get the ones stashed in my bedroom," Gabriel muttered, his eyes finding hers again, fist still knotted around his ruddy, imposing cock, the head dark purple now—engorged with blood and lust—for her.

Denny nodded, her throat still too tight for words, wondering how many women he'd taken into that bedroom—taken *in* that bedroom. The thought burned a bitter hole into her stomach, and so she settled for not worrying about it just now. Later. Later she could make herself sick with jealousy.

He stared at her for several heavy moments, knotted fist pulling long, powerful strokes over the thick mapping of veins that pulsed just beneath the silky covering of his skin, and then cut a sharp look back at Jonah, whose hands were already moving to the waistband of his slacks as he unbuckled his leather belt.

"Don't," Gabriel warned, "do anything...stupid."

"Ah, come on now, Gabe," Jonah snorted, wiping the back of his hand against his face, and then smiling at the glistening wetness that shined against his skin. "Just say what you mean. Don't hold back on my account."

"Fine. Fuck her while I'm gone and you die."

"Yeah?" Jonah laughed with a heavy, dramatic sigh. "I had a feeling you might say that."

A muttered, inaudible curse rumbled from Gabriel's lips, and Denny watched him walk away, those jeans hanging sinfully low on his hips, the long, naked line of his spine and the shifting muscles of his back making her want to growl out her claim. They made her want to run her tongue down that provocative line, nipping into the firm muscle, holding it between her teeth in a deliberate act of ownership. God, he was just so...so blatantly male, it made her hot just to look at him. And she loved him so much it hurt—more than she'd even realized before walking into this room tonight and offering up her body in an act that included her heart, as well as her soul. Loved him so much that she had no idea how she was going to survive it if he sent her out of his life come morning—but she would.

If she had to, she would survive—and do everything in her power to reach him.

Damn it, she wasn't going to just walk away and give him up. No matter what, she was *not* giving up on this man. His eyes, and those mesmerizing words, had given her an undeniable hope that she couldn't just walk away from, because his heart would give her heaven. His love would give her everything she'd ever dreamed of, and she was greedy enough to fight for it. So helplessly in love, to just walk out and leave him to his cold, aching bitterness was simply something she could not do.

She sighed, trying to hold onto the hope, determined to stay strong, and then a long, lingering lick of Jonah's tongue across her folds captured her attention. Denny moaned and looked down at him, unable to hold back an answering smile to the wicked delight curled across his devilish mouth.

"Mmm...and you wondered why I was so chipper about tonight," he teased, giving her one longer, more intimate lick that had him rooting for more of her juices in the snug clasp of her opening, before shifting to his feet in an impressive display of lean muscle and masculine grace.

She watched from heavy eyes as he shot her an outrageous wink, then unzipped those khaki slacks, shoving the expensive cloth and boxer shorts down in one smooth movement, giving her the first full look at him in all his mouthwatering glory.

"God have mercy," she choked, making him chuckle.

A sly grin kicked up one corner of that gorgeous mouth, blue eyes shining with laughter as he closed a large fist around his beautiful cock and gave it a long, hard stroke, milking a pearly drop of pre-cum at the wide tip. "Yeah, Gabe and I have more in common than one would think, considering he's a bear and I'm such an angel."

"Fallen angel, maybe," Denny whispered, unable to get over the fact that she had two drop-dead gorgeous beasts intent on lavishing her with orgasms, both of whom had the most wickedly beautiful cocks she'd ever seen. They weren't exactly the same size, but it was so damn close, she still couldn't get over it. The only significant difference she could note was that instead of Gabriel's silky black curls, Jonah had a rich patch of auburn decorating the root of his cock. His veins bulged over the dark, ruddy flesh, head crowned to a deep purple perfection, shiny and wet with the silvery drops of fluid leaking there.

He'd been so generous with her pleasure, denying his own, but she knew that wouldn't last. Before this night was over, she was going to know the feel of that cock, the taste and texture, and she couldn't form a single thought that explained how she felt about that. Nothing seemed adequate—except for maybe a lingering belief that she must have won some kind of cosmic pleasure lottery, if such a thing existed. Sexual karma? One night of forbidden pleasure to atone for all the wasted hours she'd spent beneath the fumbling hands of ineffectual lovers?

She moved to her knees, eyeing those glistening drops of pre-cum with a primal hunger that shocked her, but couldn't be denied.

Smiling his devil's smile, Jonah swiped the gleaming fluid with his thumb and then rubbed the wet pad against her bottom lip, groaning when her tongue flicked out to taste his flavor. "Mmm…" she moaned, grinning up at him. "Sweet."

"Damn," he half-laughed, half-grunted. "I'd fuck your precious face right now, Denny—just shove my cock down your tight throat and watch you suck me—but I think Gabe might kill my ass if I even try it."

She smiled up at him, moving closer to place a soft, chaste kiss against the silky, golden skin of his hipbone, his enormous cock nudging her in the shoulder, and she felt the shudder that moved through all those long, powerful muscles in his body. It made her feel drunk on power and pleasure, and with crystal clarity, she understood the thrill of what they were doing tonight. Understood precisely why those young women from their past had succumbed to the temptation of being shared by these two arrogant, dominant, utterly captivating men. She licked the crease that separated his groin from his thigh, and breathed deeply of his erotic scent, so much like Gabriel's, and yet so different. Each so wickedly seductive in his own way, and yet so much alike it was eerie.

When her face moved closer, his cock brushing her flushed cheek, Jonah fisted his hands in her long hair and pulled her away, but she could feel his hands shaking with the effort it had taken to do it, instead of holding her still and forcing that brutal erection deep into her mouth.

"Don't you trust me, Jonah?" she asked with a slow, innocent smile, blinking her eyes slowly as she ran her tongue over her bottom lip.

Jonah cursed softly. He looked down at her and shook his head, his smile crookedly endearing. "You, Denny Abbott, are a wicked little tease," he groaned, and he bent down and scooped her into his hard-muscled arms as she laughed, settling her against his chest like Rhett with his impetuous Scarlett. Denny wrapped her arms around his wide shoulders and laid her head trustingly in the crook of his neck, content to stop thinking—prepared to leave the real world behind and reap the benefits of her cosmic jackpot.

Chapter Seven

ဆာ

Gabriel walked back through the arched doorway that led from his bedroom to find his woman sprawled in the arms of his best friend, spread over Jonah's lap like a carnal feast—and the animal hunger burning in his gut perked up its ears, licking its greedy chops. He felt starved—eager to feast on more of her honeyed cream and pleasure.

Jonah lounged on the wide chair set before the far bay window with its smoked amber glass, the lights of the city glittering in an infinite shower of sparks against the covering blackness of night, and on his lap sat Denny. Her back lay to his front, shapely legs thrown over the wide arms of the chair, the demure lips of her cunt pulled open, revealing all the juice-covered beauty of the swollen pink flesh inside. Jonah's thick fingers played through her wet folds, opening her even further. Opening everything for Gabriel's hungry, devouring stare as her juices streamed, shimmering and damp against that smooth, creamy flesh.

"She's perfect, isn't she, Gabe? All ripe and wet, flushed and pink." Jonah moved one hand to pinch her swollen, pleasure-ravaged clit between two fingers. "And this poor little aching clit. She's already come so many times, and already she's pumped full again. I can even feel her heartbeat pumping inside, right here." He trailed his soaking fingers up her trembling belly, pressing his hand between her quivering breasts. "And here. It's about to thunder out of her chest."

Jonah's fingers circled first one puffy nipple, then the other, leaving a slippery trail of Denny's juices across her skin and pulling a gasping whimper from her throat, while one thick finger of his other hand delved into her slit, pressing hard and deep, stroking those tender, sensitive walls. Jonah's heavy blue eyes closed as he turned his damp face into her neck, white teeth biting at the fragile skin—and all the while she held Gabriel's darkening gaze as he stood beneath the arch, open jeans only just clutching at his hips, as if too stubborn to fall.

Damn. The head of his dick pressed wetly against his taut stomach, stiff and demanding, drumming with the need to bury itself hard and deep into that pink little hole being speared by his best friend's thick finger.

"Hell, Denny," Jonah sighed, his dark auburn head falling back against the deep green chenille throw tossed over the soft caramel leather of the chair, eyes closing as he lost himself to the pleasure of touching her, all that velvety, womanly flesh beneath his hands, his to explore. "If I'd known your pretty little pussy felt like this, sweetheart, I think I'd have been tempted to keep you all for myself."

"Not fucking likely, Jonah."

Gabriel felt his eyes narrow to mere slits as the words left his mouth, piercing with heat, but the slow, mischief-born smile hovering at the edges of Jonah's lips told him he was being jacked with again. Not that he didn't doubt Jonah would have wanted her for his own—but the arrogant ass understood precisely whom she belonged to, even if Gabriel couldn't allow himself to make that permanent claim. Understood that to have touched Denny without his permission would have ended a friendship that had now spanned more than twenty years.

Her watchful, doe-like eyes tracked him, called to him, as he began to move across the room, the plush rugs beneath his bare feet silencing his approach, leaving only the sounds of the crackling, popping fire to surround them, accompanied by her shallow, soughing breaths, and the wet sound of her desire as Jonah played his finger within the tender vise of her pussy. Her juices smoothed their way over her creamy flesh— glimmering little trails of slick, sweet fluid that Gabriel wanted to have sliding down his throat again. Wanted to feel trickling across his tongue like a soft, addictive syrup.

When he stood between her spread thighs, he could see Jonah's heavy balls wedged just beneath the lush globes of her backside, the tight sac wet with the meandering trails of her cream, and he knew the guy's cock had to be aching, nestled in that slick, sweet crack of her ass. His friend deserved to find a measure of peace, but Gabriel had no intention of letting her touch Jonah without the feel of his own hands on her body, the brutal possession of his pounding cock shoved into her as deeply as he could get.

With dark, shuttered eyes, Gabriel tossed the string of condoms he'd brought, along with an unopened tube of lube and a warm, damp washcloth, onto the small teak table positioned beside the chair. Then he leaned over and braced one hand on one of the soft leather arms, and immediately pressed one thick finger into the lush cushion of her cunt. With a thrusting movement, he added the long digit to the one Jonah had already reamed into her, and hardened his jaw at the feel of those sweet, strong muscles, so soft and slick, gripping him so perfectly.

"So damn delicate and wet. You're dripping in these pussy juices, angel," he muttered, rubbing the tip of his finger against her dewy, inner tissues, then purposefully working in a second, so that she was achingly filled with three. She grimaced, biting into her lower lip, eyes glazed with arousal and a flashing flare of pain. With a firm, savage determination, Gabriel forced them into the narrow, suctioning clench of her body, twisting inside of her, unable to get his mind around the *feel* of her. The *rightness* of being right there, with the pressure of her heartbeat surrounding his fingers, witnessing the passion rush like molten lava through those burnished, radiant eyes.

"I swear to God, Denny, you've got the tightest, sweetest little cunt I've ever felt, angel."

"Don't—" she gasped, staring up at him while a thousand different emotions flashed through her eyes. "I…I don't want to think about what…or *who* you've felt before."

Something twisted inside of him, something lonely and dark and emotionally dangerous, and he shook his head, as if he could shake it off, knowing damn well that he couldn't. Knowing it had been growing, building, breaking free of his control since the moment this woman, with her warm smiles and shining eyes, walked into his life.

"If you're talking about other women, don't waste your breath, Denny," he said, his words hard and serious, though his breath still struggled within his lungs, burning and hot. "I look at you and I can barely remember my name, much less a string of nameless faces that have meant jack to me."

"Don't…lie to me, Gabriel," she whispered past her bruised, pink lips, lowering her eyes. "You can do whatever else you want to me—just don't lie."

He withdrew his fingers from her body, and with his fist curled beneath her chin, he forced her to look back up at him. "I'm not lying, damn it," he grated through his teeth, unable to hide the ragged thread of emotion behind his words. "But for your sake, Denny, I wish to hell that I was." She opened her mouth to say something, but he cut her off, thrusting his fingers back into her clutching pussy.

"You make me forget about the past." He took a deep, rough breath, but couldn't stop. "You make me forget all the reasons why I should stay the hell away from you, and make me think about the future. That's a bad fucking road, Denny."

She appeared stunned, staring up at him in dazed surprise, but it was the frowning man at her back who broke the charged silence.

"Who says?" Jonah demanded, frowning up at him. "I say that's the best damn road you could find yourself on, Gabe. Unless you're too chicken shit to follow it."

Gabriel grunted under his breath. "Go fuck yourself."

"Ahh...now that sounds like the Gabe I know," Jonah snickered.

He cut a hard glare at the smirking redhead, knowing that Jonah was pushing him on purpose. "You think you know what's going on here?"

"I hate to say it, buddy, but I've probably got a better grip on it than you do. But fine, whatever, you just keep being a dick and telling me to fuck myself. While you're wasting your breath, I can be doing what I really want and fuck her beautiful little brains out instead."

For the second time since he'd walked back into the room, Gabriel pulled his wet fingers from her pussy, and immediately grasped Jonah's thick wrist in a powerful, biting grip, prepared to pull him free of her body. "Don't even think about it," he warned, squeezing. "You'll put your damn dick where I say you can put it."

Denny blinked up at him in some kind of worried fascination, but Jonah just snorted, and Gabriel could feel the way his best friend deliberately flexed his long finger, stretching it deep inside of her.

"Trust me, Gabe, you don't wanna know what I'm thinking about right now, or how close I am to following through on it. If you didn't have your head so far up your ass, you'd see that there's something beautiful here, and *one* of us is walking away with it at the end of the night."

The dazed look on Denny's face suddenly cleared, a small frown forming between her delicately arched brows. "I'm not an *it*," she muttered, clearly insulted.

Jonah flashed his mischievous grin, glaring a heated look at Gabriel over her shoulder. "I know, sweet stuff," he sighed, kissing her ear. "He's just pissing me off. I'm sorry. You're the most beautiful, sweetest thing I've ever touched, and," he added, blue eyes bright with challenge, "I just want to keep on touching."

"Then play nice and touch, instead of arguing," she said with a husky laugh, and just like that, the angry tension thrumming on the air settled to a low simmer, and sexual tension thickened to a strong, fiery burn.

"Yes, ma'am," Jonah chuckled with a sly, triumphant smile, and Gabriel watched as her head resettled against Jonah's broad chest. She stared back up at him, big brown eyes shimmering, the luminous color reminding Gabriel of the warm, rich, earthy browns of gleaming, polished wood—his own savage expression reflected back at him there in that brilliant surface. He breathed deeply of her fresh scent, nostrils flaring. Releasing Jonah's wrist, he dipped his fingers back inside of her, moving them in tandem with Jonah as they worked her tissues with a ruthless intent, both of them acting on the unspoken fact that she needed to be stretched before taking a cock into that tight, sweet clench.

And there was no way in hell she wasn't getting his cock.

"You look so damn pretty all covered in your cum, angel," he muttered, mesmerized by the sight of their thick penetration up the tiny, glistening mouth of her pussy. The stretched, fragile skin strained to take a width less than that of their cocks—and Gabriel knew that when he buried his dick up that drenched little slit, it was going to be so friggin' good it would probably kill him. "Do you know what it felt like when you came in my mouth? When your little cunt went so tight and hot, then rippled around my tongue, and all that sweet juice spilled down my throat? Better than sweet, Denny. Sinful. Just thinking about it makes me want to shove my face between these soft thighs and never leave."

"You're not the only one," Jonah drawled with a slow, wicked twist of his lips. The thumb he'd been scraping over her plump nipples moved to her face, rubbed that tender spot at the side of her mouth, and stroked the delicate skin.

Gabriel shot him a hard, cautioning glare. "Don't forget— you get what I say you get."

Auburn brows arched in mock surprise, making Gabriel grit his teeth. "Damn bossy tonight, Gabe," Jonah murmured. "Let's not lose sight of the fact that she's *my* gift."

"Yeah, a gift that you brought to *me*," he rasped. "*My* birthday. *My* present."

My woman.

"So then what do I get?" Jonah demanded, still purposely pushing him, Gabriel was sure. He watched as Jonah's finger plunged deep alongside his own, then carefully withdrew, rubbing through the thick, lush folds of her damp, pussy-pink cunt, the other hand drifting over her bee-stung lips, slipping just inside to stroke the tips of his fingers over her straight, white teeth. "Here...or here? And you had better decide soon, because I'm about to fucking explode."

The normally carefree lines of Jonah's face pulled tight with lust and hunger, and Gabriel knew it was time. With little effort, simply by being herself, Denny had pushed them both to the raw, brutal edge of need, just like he had always known she would. It was time to take her over the fine line they'd been carefully navigating—time to give her the full measure of what could be experienced in that oak- and cedar-scented room, the firelight flickering over their taut, sweat-slick bodies, rasping breaths and hissing logs providing a backdrop of sensual music. Hell, if they didn't cross it now, there was every chance the top of his head would come off, he was so primed.

"She's ready, Gabe. Ready to have this honeyed little pussy fucked," Jonah groaned, teasing her ripened clit as Gabriel slowly withdrew his fingers, drenched with her clean, fresh juices. As if to tempt him further—like he needed any additional fucking temptation—Jonah used both hands to pull her completely open, spreading her to expose the shy secrets within, and her arms wrapped beneath her breasts, lifting her bountiful tits up in innocent offering. She had the provocative look of a sultry centerfold, displayed there against the backdrop of Jonah's big, dark body—only Gabriel had never seen anything, either in print or in real life, that could match the sumptuous, breathtaking beauty of this woman.

His eyes tracked her sensual features, the heavy look of need in her dark eyes, and the long dark spill of her hair over Jonah's chest, before dropping his gaze to the flowering petals of her pussy. He inhaled at the sight of that slick, sweet cream easing thickly from her opening. The tender mouth nestled in all that pink flesh — gasping, tightening, so prettily swollen from the erotic play of their fingers. It was so beautifully shy, dainty, demure — and Gabriel knew he and Jonah were anything but. Christ, if he plowed fully into her to his root, like he was dying to do, there was every chance that delicate, fragile skin was going to be stretched to a point that was more pain than pleasure — and he didn't want that for her. Damn it, he wanted her screaming in ecstasy, clutching and clawing and coming all over him. Wanted to blow her mind like no other man ever had — or ever would again — not that the thought of her leaving this room tonight and letting another man touch her didn't make him violently ill, as if his heart had been ripped out of his chest and handed to him on a platter.

This entire fucking night was messing with his head — screwing with his equilibrium.

He shuddered, and an answering growl rumbled from Jonah's chest. "Stop fucking thinking about it and just do it, Gabe. Cram that gorgeous pussy full of cock and make her scream, because if you don't, man, I'm going to take my turn right now, your fucking birthday and rules be damned."

Gabriel dragged his blistering gaze away from her blossoming folds to burn another vicious warning into Jonah's challenging stare. "I don't care how many times I have to say it," he muttered, determined to keep from shouting out his claim and losing the few tattered remnants of control he'd managed to cling to. His hand cupped her warm, damp cunt, the plump cushion soft and wet against his palm, feeling as if it belonged *right* there. "This belongs to me tonight. You get it when I say you can get it."

"Then *get* the hell on with it," Jonah snarled, eyes blazing while his jaw worked, a single bead of sweat trailing down the side of his face. His dark expression hardened with raging, explosive lust, and Gabriel understood precisely what it was costing the naturally dominant man to take second chair in this unusual grouping, following his command. That right there worried him more than anything else, the fact that Jonah was willing to put himself through this. Worried him because he knew a dangerous, ulterior motive burned beneath his friend's actions. It had to be there, otherwise a man like Jonah Cartwright would have never been able to pull this off. He'd have demanded equal control, like they'd always shared back in school. No, this time was different, and the reasons were becoming increasingly clear as the night wore on and Jonah's patience wore thin.

"She's burning me alive," Jonah bit out, glaring up at him, "and I don't wanna explode 'til I'm inside. As fucking deep inside as I can get."

"You want inside?" Gabriel rumbled, distantly aware that Denny was watching him with a bemused expression on her flushed face, clearly intrigued by the possessive battle being waged between them over the possession of her pleasure. "Fine, Jonah. But you get in when and where I say." Standing straight, he held out his hand to the woman responsible for the twisting in his heart and cock, scared shitless of where this was all going to lead, but unable to keep from rushing headlong into the terrifying unknown. "Give me your hand, Denny," he ordered, ignoring the infuriating tremble in his fingers.

She blinked up at him, a soft, siren smile floating over those lush lips—the same smile she'd given him a hundred times since walking into his life—and his heart seemed to churn within his chest. It gave her the appearance of a wicked angel, with her face flushed and damp, lips rosy from the pounding of his cock. *His Denny.* She was innocence and sin all wrapped up in the most intoxicating package he could have ever imagined.

And with that spellbinding trust that made his gut cramp, his heart ache, shimmering there in those beautiful brown eyes, she placed her small, delicate fingers in his palm, handing over more than her body in the simple gesture. He knew it—could see it there in that temptingly vibrant gaze—but ground his jaw and stubbornly refused to fall into it.

Gabriel pulled her to her feet in a sudden, jerking move that had her tumbling into his chest, then quickly—goddamn it, it had to be quickly before he got lost in that dangerous emotion-filled look in her eyes—turned her toward Jonah, pulling her back to his front, one thick arm secured around her waist to lock her in place. With his free hand, he stroked the feminine line of her spine, luxuriating in the delicate silk of her warm, velvety skin, then gently pushed down between her shoulder blades, bending her at the waist—pushing her head toward his best friend's waiting cock.

And Jonah wasn't kidding about being ready to burst. His hard-on surged up from his body like a granite-hard spike, the broad, fat head trailing glistening lines of pre-cum down its sides, dark skin pulsing with the heavy flow of blood through that thick network of veins. Denny's arms shot forward to catch herself, though Gabriel kept her secure with his arm at her waist. She braced her slim hands on the first available surface, which just happened to be Jonah's tense, parted thighs, and the shining hair trailing over her shoulder brushed against the desperate, bulging head of his dick, pulling a strangled sound from Jonah's throat.

"Now suck his cock, angel." Gabriel kept his voice low, soothing, yet crisp with command, knowing instinctively that she loved giving into him as much as he loved controlling her. At least here—in sex. Beyond that, he just gloried in the warm, giving, breathtaking woman she was—knowing that he'd feel unworthy of her until the day he died. But tonight—when it came to her physical satisfaction—he loved taking charge and commanding her pleasure. Loved molding something so inherently primal and wild from the pure innocence of her need. And he'd witnessed enough of her pleasure-rich responses beneath his hands and mouth to know that she craved the exact same thing.

"I'm going to eat some more of this honeyed little pussy, feel your hot, sweet juices fill my mouth, spill over my tongue, swallow them down my throat, and when I can't take it anymore, I'm going to pound my cock into this dainty little hole, Denny. All of it. You demanded it, angel, so I won't hold back. I'm going to fuck you with everything I have, and when I'm done, I'm going to take you again," he groaned, his harsh voice filled with the vicious, brutal need that he couldn't disguise. "It won't stop—so you had better fucking remember that when I'm pounding you through that goddamn chair, just like you've begged me to."

"I don't remember begging," she gasped, and he could hear the mischievous smile in her voice.

"Oh yes you have," he laughed in a low, strained rumble. "Every time you set those big brown eyes on me, you're begging me to fuck you, Denny. To give it to you as hard and deep as I can. Don't even try to deny it, angel. I could nail you to the damn wall with my dick, right in the middle of the office for everyone to see, and you'd still beg me for more."

She moaned an excited, throaty whisper of sound in response, rolling her spine beneath him in a pleading, provocative arc, and he watched as Jonah took his thick cock into his fist, and nudged the flared tip against her mouth.

"Let me in, Denny," Jonah rasped. "Let me watch you suck me while Gabe stuffs your little pussy full of cock. As much as you can take—until he tells me to leave—remember? We're both going to be filling all these perfect, pink, pretty little holes. Packing you full, sweet stuff. Everywhere. Now open up and suck my dick like a good little birthday present."

She gave a soft, husky laugh, and Gabriel had to bite back the need to spin her around and swallow that sweet, somehow innocent sound down his throat in one violent, hungry gulp. "I would, but...it's not your birthday, Mr. Cartwright," she teased, breathless, and despite the internal, thundering battle being waged from his mind to his balls, Gabriel couldn't help but smile at her playfulness.

"We'll fucking pretend it is then, Denny," Jonah groaned. "Pretend it's the goddamn Fourth of July for all I care, but suck my cock before I die, here."

With the urgent need to taste her delicate flesh beneath his lips, Gabriel pushed her hair completely to the side and pressed his open mouth to the vulnerable, silken skin at the nape of her neck. She arched beneath him as he bent his knees and pressed forward, so that his cock wedged itself within the warm, sweet cleft of her ass cheeks, knowing that the coarse denim of his jeans, the stubborn cloth still just clutching at his hips, would feel strangely alluring against her silky flesh. She moaned, wriggling her hips, rubbing that lush, rosy bottom that he ached to pound the hell out of against him, nearly making his eyes cross.

He looked over her shoulder, at the way his best friend's cock nudged at her lips, and whispered, "Now I know how Jonah felt, Denny."

She moaned at his rasped words, and Jonah cursed under his breath, his blue eyes rapt as he watched Denny begin to work her magic on the swollen head of his cock. A part of Gabriel's brain told him it wasn't right—that he should be pissed—but the sight of her sucking on Jonah was so brutally erotic, he had to grit his teeth to keep from plowing into her right then and there. He would have, damn it—would have been crammed to the hilt in that pretty pussy—but he wanted this to last. Wanted to drag it out for as long as he could, gorging himself on as much of her as he could get, soaking her into his system—knowing it was going to friggin' kill him when it was over and he no longer had her under his hands, his to touch…to eat…to fuck, the way she was meant to be.

Just his—entirely fucking his.

With rasping strokes of his tongue and nipping bites of his teeth, he worked his way down the smooth, sensuous line of her spine until he reached that delectable backside, and sank his teeth into the full, womanly flesh at the exact moment he felt her move forward, taking more of Jonah's cock into her mouth.

His best friend gave a rough, roaring grunt of satisfaction. Jonah's body jerked hard beneath her, pressing her back against him, and Gabriel smiled against that sweet flesh, licking his way down the even sweeter cleft, lapping at the rich juices streaming from her pussy, until he found her snug vulva and pierced it with a hard, hungry thrust of his tongue. And all the while, he sank slowly to his knees behind her, the pain in his left knee blissfully lost somewhere beneath the mind-shattering pleasure he found in her taste.

"Ahh, that's better," he growled, eyes narrowed as he studied all of her, everything right there for him to see. "I want you to come for me again, Denny. Just like this." She wiggled her ass, pushing her drenched little pussy in his face, and he smiled. "That's it, angel," he groaned, licking her sweet cunt lips, soft and so temptingly tender, like slick, wet silk. "Feed me some more of this beautiful pussy and fuck my mouth while Jonah fucks yours, Denny. Come on…shove this pretty little thing in my face and ride my tongue. Let me feel you come around it."

Over the harsh, erratic pounding of his heart, Gabriel could hear Jonah growling, cursing, as she sucked him off, and it only added to the thick, voluptuous pulse of lust pumping through his veins. He plunged his tongue deep into her clinging, silken little slit, and she clamped down on him so sweetly, he nearly lost it. Could see the huge, irrevocable loss of control looming in the distance, towering on the horizon, with no means of stopping. And just like that, he was caught, trapped, and he couldn't have pulled away from her if his life depended on it.

Gabriel ate at her, starved for the feel and taste, unable to get deep enough into that tight, delicious little hole. She fluttered around his plunging strokes, and all it took was one swipe of his thumb over her swollen clit, and she broke, her muscles milking his tongue in a strong, steady rhythm as her climax poured through her and her precious, honeyed cream spilled into his mouth. He swallowed again and again, wanting all of it, demanding it, taking more and more, while she wiggled and shimmied against his face.

And as her low, hoarse cries broke from her throat, muffled against his best friend's rigid flesh, Gabriel knew that he'd made a fatal error here tonight, but refused to admit it.

Knew that he'd passed some predetermined point of no return.

Knew that he'd never—*never*—no matter how much he took, be able to get enough of this one, intoxicating, sexy sweet woman.

Chapter Eight

ᔥ

Blindly—Denny's addictive taste still sweet in his throat—Gabriel found himself reaching out for the condoms, snagging one foil packet to rip open and roll over the throbbing, raging ache of his cock.

"Shit, Gabe, you should've seen her face," Jonah grunted, deep voice ragged and on edge. "The second you started eating her out, these big brown eyes nearly rolled back in her head. Beautiful, man. I can't wait to see what she looks like when you get your dick in and finally start fucking her. Can't wait to hear her screaming around my cock when she comes."

Denny's head lifted, tossed, sending the long, silken wash of her hair rushing down the curved line of her spine in a heavy, mahogany fall that gleamed against the pale, buttery softness of her skin.

"I've never had a man make me scream before," she moaned in a halting, throaty rasp, as if having to work the words out past the tightness of her throat, over the jagged panting of her breath. Looking over her shoulder, she shot a hot, meaningful look at him that had his damn heart doing a backflip into his stomach. Her pink little tongue flicked out to lick at that plump lower lip, and then she smiled. Fucking smiled at him, and it nearly made his cock explode—nearly sent him spewing into the miserable, dick-choking latex before he'd even gotten the damn thing inside of her. "I'd like…" she swallowed, panting, "I *want* that man to be you, Gabriel. I want you to be the one who makes me scream."

"You want my cock, Denny? You're gonna get it, beautiful," he promised roughly, rising back over her until he could nip at one delicate lobe, the warm, lush taste of her skin making him feel drunk with pleasure, those sexy words slamming through his system with an emotional punch that nearly knocked him on his ass. They made his head feel thick—his dick feel like it'd rip itself open, it was so full of blood, lust and brutal, relentless need. "But don't ever say I didn't warn you, angel."

She turned back to Jonah, laughing, saying, "And I already told you how I feel about your *warnings*, Mr. Harrison."

He bit down on the side of her throat, carefully nipping in a primal act of dominance, wanting to brand her as his own. "Yeah," he mouthed against the moist heat of her skin, "but then you weren't crammed full of my hungry cock at the time, sweetheart, getting this pretty little pussy fucked apart, were you?"

She shivered beneath him, a deep, readying breath filling her lungs—but he couldn't do it. Despite his harsh words, Gabriel was still afraid of hurting her, and so he didn't shove himself in with the force of a battering ram, though God knew he wanted to. No—he tormented her...and him. Just settled himself against that tiny opening, those petal-soft inner lips kissing the hot head of his dick, and began a gentle thrusting motion that worked him slowly—*ever so fucking slowly*—inside. He rocked against the lush cushion of her ass, stretching her in excruciatingly unhurried degrees, until her hands were pounding on the soft chenille at Jonah's sides, her gasps muffled by the thick cock once again driving into her mouth. Jonah had his head thrown back, eyes squeezed shut, jaw locked tight while the heavy fists he had knotted in her hair, holding her face over him, worked her over the top part of his cock again and again.

Her hips wiggled, frantic as she struggled to take more of the burgeoning flesh impaling her pussy, but Gabriel refused to give it to her, still shafting her slowly, bit by bit, mesmerized by the erotic sight of that tender, demure flesh stretching open around him, tight and straining from his thick, brutal penetration. Her rich cream eased his way, slipping out to soak him like warm, wet silk, and he cursed the damn rubber that kept him from feeling it against the hot, naked skin of his dick.

Suddenly, she shouted around Jonah's thrusting cock, and the redhead allowed her to pull back, only for a moment, just long enough for her to snarl, "Stop teasing me, Gabriel! Don't be a bastard!"

A harsh, booming sound of happiness burst past Gabriel's lips, the sound so foreign, he barely recognized it. She honestly made him...*happy*—even while tearing him apart—and he couldn't recall the last time he'd felt that crisp, rushing burst of emotion. Shit, he knew without a doubt that he'd never felt like he did at this moment—so full with the knowledge of a woman while he penetrated her and became a part of her body, as if she'd slipped under his skin, laying claim to everything within. "I'm not teasing you, angel," he croaked out of a tight throat, still shaking with laughter.

"Like hell you aren't," she muttered, running her tongue down the side of Jonah's cock, taking a nip of the fat, heavy head that had the other man moaning, jerking beneath them. Gabriel watched as she licked her way up the thick vein running down its center, knowing she could feel the pulse of Jonah's blood as it drummed against her tongue, mirroring the pulse of her sweet cunt around the slow pumping of his cock. "Don't stop. Not now. Don't stop...fucking me," she moaned, dragging her open mouth over Jonah's gleaming skin, her voice a throaty plea for *more*—for *everything*. "Don't hold back."

"I have to." His jaw clenched so hard he was amazed his teeth didn't crack. "You're too damn tiny, Denny. I'll hurt you if I let myself forget that and pound this snug little cunt the way I'm dying to."

"*Nooo*," she gasped, groaning, her swollen lips like a bruised pink promise of pleasure against the glistening head of Jonah's bulging cock. "I don't need you to be careful—all I need is for you to make me scream." And then she wiggled that gorgeous ass, managing to grasp onto another thick inch of his dick before he dug his fingers into her hips, knowing he'd leave their imprint upon her delicate skin, but somehow unable to loosen his hold, as though his brain was no longer transmitting signals to his body. "Come on," she drawled, her husky voice whispering through his head, drugging his reason. "I *dare* ya."

And he did — *had to* — because he was helpless to defy her pleading demand. Faintly aware of that distant part of his mind shouting out its caution, Gabriel tensed his muscles and rammed unforgivably hard, slamming her into Jonah, battling through her clenching resistance with the primitive, brutal cramming of his heavy cock into that drenched little hole. With the harsh, roaring shout of a warrior, he forced his way through those narrow walls as he shoved inside that wet, clinging heat, jabbing his hips to work himself in, knowing he had to be hurting her as the keening cries and feral screams ripped out of her throat each time she took another inch, the wrenching sounds washing over Jonah's pulsing flesh.

Gabriel locked his jaw, teeth gnashing, unable to believe what it felt like sinking into her. Sinking, thrusting…and then finally giving in and hammering his thick flesh through her squeezing muscles so hard it nearly toppled the fucking chair, sending them all sprawling to the floor in a tangle of limbs, pounding cocks and mouthwatering pussy. He'd never felt anything so mind-shatteringly perfect, so tight and wet, the searing, slick heat of her liquid sheath clutching at him like a narrow throat. It pulled the pleasure up out of him, from the soles of his feet to his scalp, all of it being suctioned into the root of his cock, pulled free from the painfully tight hole in the heavy head that spewed small bursts of fluid as he struggled to hold back the flood.

With narrowed eyes, he watched from over her shoulder as she moved deeper over Jonah's cock, and the bastard smiled at her, all tenderness and caring, his thumb rubbing the corner of her stretched, swollen lips. "That's a good girl, Denny," Jonah rasped. "Ah, sweet stuff, you suck cock like you were made for it. So beautiful—my dick shafting this screaming little hole of a mouth while Gabe packs that precious cunt so full."

"Christ—she's incredible, isn't she, Jonah?"

"I think she's amazing," his friend gritted through his teeth, watching Denny go at his cock with wild eyes, the blue bright and blistering, the muscles in his neck pulled tight as he struggled not to come. He looked drugged with pleasure, and Gabriel knew exactly how he felt. He could see it there in every hard, tight tendon, the sinewy forearms taut as Jonah released her hair to grip onto the arms of the chair, holding on as if he'd slip right off the edge of a cliff were he to let go.

Damn woman had them both twisted up into knots.

"There's something about her mouth that feels so...different...isn't there?" he groaned, pulling back and then punctuating his words with a hard, slamming stroke of his cock that crammed the head of his dick so deep, she showered Jonah in another scream. "Like you're fucking into some kind of paradise. A white-hot cloud, so soft...even innocent, and yet so unbelievably wicked it makes you want to come all over her. I can't believe it—but this sweet little pussy feels even better.

"Do you like that, Denny?" he whispered roughly in her ear, the heat of his chest pressed to her back as he surrounded her with his body, working his heavy shaft into her harder...and harder, jolting her with his powerful strokes. He knew she had to be sore, but he was without mercy, defeated by his own desperate hunger. "Do you like knowing how far you can push us, how hard you can make us ache? And it isn't easy, angel. We've seen too much, done too much, to fall apart like this. You're like a little witch casting her spell over us."

She sucked down on Jonah's cock like a sensual goddess, her jaws and throat working, pulling a snarling, animal sound from Jonah's parted lips. "Yeah, I can tell that you like it.

That's it, angel. Suck him like you sucked on me. Let him feel how incredible you are."

"Aw, hell," Jonah muttered, working his jaw. "Goddamn it, I have to come. *Now,*" he growled, looking at Gabriel, obviously asking for permission in an act that chafed at his own dominant needs to do with Denny however the hell he pleased.

And it hit Gabriel out of nowhere, the sudden realization that he didn't want Jonah flooding Denny's mouth with his cum. Didn't want another man's release flowing down her throat, becoming a part of her. With a coarse, blistering snarl of sound, he found himself pulling out of her clenching pussy, the tight, sopping tissues making a wet, protesting sound that mirrored Denny's startled yelp. Jonah's dark eyes drilled into him, taunting him with the burning question of where he wanted this to go next, as if he had a fucking clue.

It made him want to roar. Made him want to pick something up and hurl it against the wall—the way this terrifying feeling of possession, of ownership, kept locking its teeth into his jugular, demanding he recognize and accept its existence. His dick was ready to strangle him for leaving the sheer perfection of her body, but that dark, clawing part of him breaking open deep inside was adamant. It didn't want Jonah's cum inside of her, flowing into her belly, mixing with his own. No matter what happened at the end of the night, he wanted...*needed*...that one possessive mark on her to be his and his alone. It was so intimate, so raw, and he was a big enough bastard to demand it for himself.

Hell, he didn't have any choice. Something stubborn and defiant in his chest demanded it. Something he was afraid to look at too closely.

Curling his hand around her neck in a gentle hold, Gabriel ran one palm down her slim throat, feeling the muscles work as she continued to suck at his best friend's shaft. "Not here," he ordered, and it was a guttural command.

Jonah snorted, blue eyes flashing, so hot they should have seared his flesh. "Dickhead."

Gabriel's smile was sharp and hard. "Yeah, that's not the first time you've called me that," he replied, pulling Denny away from Jonah's pumping cock. Damn, the guy really did look like he was going to explode, the flared head of his dick dark and slick, bruised with need.

"Won't be the last time either," Jonah gritted through his teeth, using one hand to fist around the thick root of his cock, fingers squeezing to hold in his cum, while Denny moved forward to lash the top inches with that wicked little tongue, making him tremble beneath her.

With a firm grip on her hips, Gabriel turned her and lifted her up onto the bastard's lap, refusing to meet her questioning gaze. With a quick flick of his wrist, he viciously ripped off another condom, then tossed it at the suddenly grinning redhead.

"Oh, hell, it's about damn time," Jonah laughed, his hand shooting out to catch the flying arc of glittering foil, and while he rolled the thin condom on, Gabriel pulled off the one still choking his dick. It pissed him off to do it, but he knew he had to get it together before he allowed himself to come inside of her. With quick, efficient movements, he grabbed the warm washcloth and wiped the sticky lube from the latex off his cock, then tossed the cloth back onto the table and allowed his hungry gaze to find Denny's.

Her eyes were bright and wide, full of questions, and yet so trusting it made him want to rail at her. Made him want to shake her until he could get it through her thick little head that was he was a bastard and didn't deserve her trust, or the pleasure of her body, or any of those other terrifying, heart-wrenching emotions he could see shining there in the luminous depths of those big brown eyes, her long lashes spiky and damp, glistening with tears.

Hardening his jaw, hands clenched into fists at his sides, he ripped his gaze from hers and cut a hard look at Jonah, who sat watching him with the starving urgency of a captive being allowed their first sip of water after days of deprivation.

"Go ahead," he muttered, jerking his chin at them. "Put your dick in her, Jonah. Fill up that tight little cunt while I watch."

The words hadn't even finished leaving his mouth before Jonah had his big hands clasped onto her hips and was lifting her high over his rigid erection. He lowered her with a guttural, hissing sound of anticipation, and then the head of his dick pressed just inside those cherry inner lips of her pussy, and they both groaned. Denny bit her bottom lip, her straight white teeth digging into the plump, glossy flesh, but she never tore her trusting stare from Gabriel's face, and it drove him mad.

He ground his jaw, fisting his hands tighter to keep from grabbing her to him and running as hard and fast as he could, until there was a chance in hell he could outrun his demons...his past...his fears.

She panted, squirming within Jonah's grip, and he could see the pleasure rising through her as Jonah pushed up higher into her body, his friend's thick cock penetrating the pussy of *his woman*. His throat worked as he swallowed, almost too tight for words, but he finally managed to say, "Tell me how it feels, Denny."

She shook her head, wetting her lips. "I...I can't," she whispered.

Jonah growled at her words, and began working himself in, pulling her down with a slow, steady pressure, and she trembled, panting, bracing her upper body with her hands on his spread knees, her bent legs on the outside of his muscular thighs.

"Tell me how it feels, Denny," Gabriel repeated. His voice was quiet, low, and yet she flinched as if he'd shouted at her. He lifted one hand to his dick and began stroking the hungry, angry flesh as he watched Jonah pressing deeper and deeper inside of her, the delicate inner lips of her cunt stretched wide again to accommodate his thick width. "I want to know, Denny. Tell me."

"H-h-hot," she panted, arching her upper body, her head now tilted back on her fragile neck in order to be able to look up at his face, he stood so close.

"Go on," he rasped. "Talk to me. I love to hear that little catch in your voice when you're getting fucked."

"Thick," she said, dragging her bottom lip through her teeth, eyes so wide they were nearly round, drowning in pleasure. "Full," she added. "Hard."

Jonah made a deep, animal sound in the back of his throat, and his hips suddenly jerked, forcing her to take him completely to the root. Gabriel watched, tight-jawed, as the shocked pleasure-pain washed over her precious face with such honest emotion, all of it right there for him to see. It was as if looking through a window into her soul.

"And I know just how you feel to Jonah, angel. Tight, wet, clutching at him. You're like a hungry little mouth that wants to swallow him whole. You have the kind of pussy made for a man to fuck, Denny. He puts his dick in and you squeeze down around him so damn sweetly, it makes him feel like an animal and he just wants to slam you against a wall and pound you 'til neither one of you can stand."

She ground herself down on Jonah, making him gasp and groan at her back, and a small smile curled shyly across her mouth, her long, beautiful hair streaming down her back, and Gabriel knew she was the most desirable woman he'd ever seen in his entire life.

"You like that thought, don't you, angel? You like knowing the power you hold over us, huh? How hard we get just looking at you. How badly we just want to worship at your pretty little feet. You like it, don't you, Denny?"

Her smile faltered, brows drawing together, tits quivering as Jonah's long fingers bit into her hips and began working her on his cock, harder, faster, both of them gasping and wet, sweat slicking across their bodies like a fine mist, shimmering in a wash of gold beneath the flickering firelight. "I don't want to be worshipped," she groaned. "I...I just want to be—"

"What, Denny?" He moved closer, his naked dick only inches from the glossy, bruised silk of her lips, and he had to clench his fists tighter to keep from grabbing her head and forcing her mouth back onto his cock. "What do you want?"

"Nothing," she panted as Jonah worked her harder, pumping his hips, cramming his thick cock up into her as he brought her down on him again and again while a low, steady stream of erotic curses fell from his lips, guttural and raw.

Gabriel dared her to look away from him as he moved just that fraction forward. The gleaming, fat head of his dick nudged her cheek, but she held his narrow-eyed stare, proud and beautiful and so fucking important to him, it scared the shit out of him. He breathed deeply through his nose, taking her warm scent into his head, and smeared his dripping cock head over her delicate cheekbone, down her throat, painting her gorgeous tits with the glistening trail of his sex juice, his damn dick leaking like it was about to let go in a flood of cum.

"Beautiful," he murmured, and a sudden flash of longing so deep and emotionally powerful filled her eyes that he couldn't stop his sharp intake of breath. She blinked, lashes glistening in the firelight, and started to turn her head away from what she saw on his face, but he reached out and caught her chin in his fingers, forcing her to look up at him. "Answer me," he suddenly demanded. "What the hell do you want?"

"Everything!" she rasped, her expression turning mutinous, and yet, he could see the hurt rushing through her now, hear it lashing out at him with her words. "This, damn it. I want *this*. I just want to get fucked. Isn't that what you want to hear?" she all but snarled up at him, and he felt the earth shift beneath his feet, heart threatening to thunder out of his chest.

"Then you'll get as much as you can take." The rough words were scraped out of his throat while he dropped to his knees, watching her eyes go wide as he moved in on her. "Just like Jonah said. How much can you take, Denny?"

Her chin lifted, but her eyes were going wild with the pleasure Jonah kept pumping into her, the lust burning swift and bright alongside the anger. "I…I hate to break it to you," she panted, a deep, dark flush moving up over her swaying breasts, her throat, "but I'm not afraid of you, Gabriel Harrison."

"No?" he smiled, already lowering his head to run the flat of his tongue over one swollen, blushing pink nipple, his gut burning with satisfaction when she cried out. "We'll see just how brave you are, Denny, before tonight is over."

And then he drew her into the hot, liquid heat of his mouth. She moaned, arching hard, forcing her breast deeper into his mouth as he opened and took in as much of her as he could, loving the feel and taste of her succulent flesh, knowing he'd never be able to get his fill.

"Oh Christ…every time you suck on her tit," Jonah grunted at her back, "she clamps down on my dick like a fist. Like a greedy little hand."

Gabriel moved to her other breast, trailing his mouth over her moist skin, addicted to the hot taste of desire sizzling on her lush curves, and wet her nipple with the tip of his tongue, loving the way she squirmed, gasping. Her hands lifted to fist in his short hair, trying to pull him closer, and he felt utterly at her mercy, as if she somehow held all the power…all the control.

"Please," she moaned, pushing her breast against his lips. "Please," she begged through that plump, fragile mouth, looking down at him, her hair falling around them like a veil while she jolted with Jonah's savage strokes up into her body. "*Please…*"

"Please, what?" he whispered, letting his breath tickle the wet tip of her nipple.

"Suck on me," she moaned, eyes bright with hunger...with need...*with love!*

His gut cramped, but he couldn't look away this time, couldn't rip his gaze from that beautiful emotion swirling there in the shimmering depths of her eyes. He opened and took her in, suckling at her breast while her soft hands found his cheeks, holding his face in the tender cradle of her palms, and his eyes went dangerously hot.

Fuck no! he silently snarled, ripping away from her.

She opened her mouth, but whatever she would have said was lost beneath Jonah's rumbling growl, and Gabriel watched with a strange, twisting pain in his gut as Jonah's right hand moved around to her front, dipping between her splayed thighs, his fingers capturing her ripe, red little clit in their clever tips and plucking at the swollen nub.

She shook, planting her hands against his knees again as he began to work her clit and cunt with an intensity that left her breathless, the delicate flush on her breasts going a deep, dark, violent red, and Gabriel knew she was getting ready to come yet again, just as they'd promised.

"I can't—*oh god*—I'll die," she moaned, fighting it this time. She bit her lip, hard enough to draw blood, while the air filled with their frantic breaths and slapping flesh.

"Oh hell," Jonah grunted, throwing back his head as his left hand clenched tighter at her hip, knuckles going white against the rosy glow of her skin. "You're so damn sweet, Denny, I can't stand it," he muttered, jamming up into her. "I wanted to come the second I got my dick in you, like some short-triggered teenager."

"Hear what you do to him, Denny?" Gabriel murmured, unable to rip his gaze away from the erotic sight of their pumping bodies, the air going warm and musky with the earthy smells of sex and lust. "Do you have any idea how hard it is to get him like that, the depraved bastard that he is?" he asked with another hard smile, his lips feeling tight, while the head of his cock pulsed against his abdomen, ready to kill him. "Do you?"

She shook her head, wetting her lips as Jonah tunneled in and out of her creamy cunt, the tender, silken inner lips quivering with strain—and it was suddenly happening again, everything buzzing inside of him, all the intimate little details of her. Her face, her mouth, the way he could see her heart right there in those tear-damp eyes.

Before he knew what he was doing, Gabriel stumbled to his feet, ready to back away, run, not really knowing why or where he was heading, but she reached out to him. Her small hands grabbed at his hips, clutching and damp as she shoved at his open jeans, and before he could blink, she had that hot little mouth clamped around his dick, sucking him in, and it was like being punched in the stomach, nearly doubling him over. She came at the first touch of his cock head against her tongue, her lips quivering around his burning flesh, hoarse cries vibrating against his hard shaft, while Jonah growled at her back, obviously doing everything he could to hold off his release—just a little longer—desperate to make it last.

Not that he could blame him.

Gabriel tunneled his shaking hands into the silken, luxurious mass of her hair, holding her head, and his breath choked in his lungs, every muscle in his body going hard with the ecstasy of having a part of him inside of her again. It felt so goddamn right and wrong—like a sinful pleasure that you knew was going to land you equally in heaven and hell. His stomach tightened as he threw back his head, gnashing his teeth to keep from crying out at the raging, merciless pleasure.

She stumbled through an awkward rhythm, with Jonah still pounding up into her, even harder now, jarring her with his heavy, brutal strokes, but her lack of skill didn't take away from the perfection of the moment. Her lips were soft, damp around the burning heat of his skin, her tongue wicked and wanting as it lashed at him, licking and stroking, while her cheeks sucked in, pulling him deeper. It was always like this, each time he got anywhere inside of her, like jacking himself into a live current of electricity. Every inch of his skin tingled, buzzing from the soles of his feet up to the top of his head — ears hot, eyes stinging and wet, throat tight while his chest heaved.

He couldn't hold it. His spine tingled, cock surging, balls pulling tight, and then he was pumping into her hot little mouth, shooting his cum down the back of her throat. She struggled, but didn't let up, sucking at him until she'd pulled every blistering drop from the pulsing head of his dick for the second time that night, and he nearly died, choking on the telling words that he wanted to let go, shouting them out into the warm, thick air.

But it was another voice that rang out, feral and wild. "My turn now," Jonah growled. "Are you ready, Denny? I'm going to come so hard, sweet stuff. If it weren't for this damn rubber, I'd fucking fill you up."

She cried out as Gabriel pulled himself from her mouth, head shaking as her tongue swiped her lower lip, catching a gleaming drop of cum. He swallowed, hard, wondering why steam didn't come from his ears, he was so turned on, even after having poured himself down her throat.

He struggled out of his jeans and dropped to his knees again, hard enough that he banged his knee, but it didn't matter. Nothing mattered, except being close to her. She blinked at him, those lush lips quivering while he caught her splayed legs behind her knees and pulled them out, high and wide, so that he stretched open the puffy lips of her pussy as he pushed her back against Jonah. In this new position, he could see all of it, all of her, everything happening there between her legs, with perfect, gut-clawing detail. Jonah pressed forward, supporting her back with his broad chest, and Gabriel lowered his head between her wide thighs, watching the erotic sight of Jonah's thick dick pumping up into her tiny, dainty hole, breathing deeply of her sweet scent mixed with Jonah's muskier heat. He pressed closer, and with the flat of his tongue, he lashed the hard, ravaged little bud of her clit at the top of her sex, and she sobbed out a hoarse, frantic sound, digging her fingers into his hair.

"*Gabriel*," she cried, his name strangled in her chest, and he wanted to throw his arms around her and shove his tongue down her throat, hearing her shout his name into his mouth. But he couldn't do it—he couldn't kiss her—no matter how damn badly he wanted to. She'd pull the truth right up out of him with that sweet, tender mouth that he knew would taste of promises and hope, and he'd be wide open, unmasked and vulnerable, completely at her mercy.

He drew a deep, shuddering breath into his lungs, and was filled again with the sumptuous scents of her warm pussy juices and cum as they washed over Jonah. Gabriel swiped at her clit again, and again, tickling it with the tip of his tongue, then rubbing it, letting her feel the gentle scratch of its surface, and all the while Jonah's hard cock jabbed into her with short, powerful thrusts. He kept his face buried there between her legs, his tongue on the pulse of her clit, dangerously close to his best friend's cock as it hammered into *his woman* – and Gabriel savagely claimed ownership of her pleasure...even as Jonah started to come.

Chapter Nine

ଈ

Denny struggled, thrashing under the mind-shattering bliss, but she couldn't find herself in that destructive world, where Gabriel mercilessly lashed her clit and the fat, flared tip of Jonah's cock head surged against tissues so sensitive...so deep inside of her, that she sobbed from each pump of his hips as he scraped over them. He came with as much feral violence and power as she had known he would, growling in her ear, before setting his teeth into her shoulder and marking her.

She writhed between them, another orgasm bubbling up inside of her, if the others had ever even ended. She felt as if she were riding a towering, terrifying wave of ecstasy that never crashed, but just kept going, building and building until she couldn't think, couldn't breathe, could only feel. Jonah's evil fingers found her breasts, torturing her nipples with pleasure, snarling against the flesh he held between his teeth when the play at her breasts made her cunt contract around him even tighter, probably bruising his shaft. And all the while, Gabriel destroyed her clit, merciless in his drive to once again push her over the edge...of reason...sanity...everything.

When the crest of the orgasm hit her, it was like dying, everything white and black and splashed with brilliant, blinding light. She drowned and flew, spinning and sinking, feeling pummeled as if in the center of a spiraling tornado, pulled under the churning waves of the sea—and yet, it was heaven, her body pulsing on wave after agonizing wave of indescribable rapture. Each time, she just kept coming harder...and then harder, until her body felt battered and boneless. Something soft and vulnerable that could be twisted and molded into whatever form they chose to create next, and her inner wild woman purred her pleasure.

By the time she opened her eyes, Denny had no idea how long they'd stayed like that, limbs tangled, skin sticky with sweat, her body mashed between them at the edge of the mammoth chair like some kind of twisted modern sculpture. She felt Gabriel's hard cock against her thigh, the thick stalk already pumped and eager for another go, and it was almost frightening, the speed with which desire raced beneath the surface of her skin, like a brushfire feeding off of gasoline.

"You fucking killed me," Jonah grated against her shoulder, kissing the possessive mark of his teeth in her skin, lapping at it with his tongue like a big, gorgeous jungle cat, making her shiver. He pressed his wet forehead into her neck while Gabriel nuzzled the base of her throat, and she struggled to find her breath. "I don't think I've ever come so hard, Denny. Never. You are one scary broad, you know that, sweet stuff?"

"M-m-me?" she stammered, surprised that she could still find the energy to giggle. "What did *I* do?"

"You're just you," Jonah sighed, running his big, rough hands over her sides one last time, before falling back into the chair. "Just sweet, beautiful Denny."

She felt one blunt finger trail down the damp line of her spine, and there was a strange longing in that simple caress that told her this had meant something to him, even though tonight was meant for Gabriel. That told her she had touched this man in some special way, and her heart skipped a beat at the strange, wonderful knowledge.

His cock pulsed inside of her, and she caught her breath at the delicious ripple of pleasure it rocketed through her overly sensitive tissues, and then Gabriel wrapped his arms around her back, her breasts crushed against the naked beauty of his broad, muscle-sculpted chest. He lifted her from his best friend's lap, and Jonah's heavy cock pulled free from her body with a wet pop of sound that almost made her smile.

She was weak, drunk on the steady beat of bliss drumming through her veins, content to stay within the circle of Gabriel's arms forever. He leaned down and pressed a soft, urgent kiss to the corner of one eye, trailing the rough silkiness of his lips down the side of her face, beneath her ear, and she shifted, trying to capture his mouth, but he pulled away...intentionally evading her.

He did not want to kiss her mouth.

Oh god. Denny's insides twisted, but she struggled not to dwell on how that little denial could hurt so damn badly.

She hid her face against his chest, understanding exactly what this meant. Gabriel was willing to give her his body — but he would not give her his heart.

Jonah's kisses had been addictive, playful, like foreplay, but she knew instinctively what the touch of Gabriel's scarred mouth against her own would do. But he didn't want that. Wasn't willing to share that part of himself with her, and for the brief flash of a moment, she considered breaking free of his embrace, and running, only she had nowhere to run to. An empty apartment? A life that had been put on hold, while her heart yearned for something it would never have?

She was in hell, the traitorous organ aching, and yet, this was still heaven, if not a bittersweet one, being held in his strong arms, her ear pressed to the thundering cadence of his heart. She moved to press a tender, longing kiss over that erratic pounding, when he turned her in his arms, facing her toward Jonah once again. That beautiful, auburn-haired male watched her with blue eyes the color of smoldering sapphires, dark and still hungry, a small, mischievous smile curving the corner of his mouth, while Gabriel ran his big, hot hands up and down her sides, over her breasts, his touch claiming possession.

"As much as you can take, Denny," Jonah murmured, when her gaze fell to his condom-covered, half-hard cock. Her gaze lifted, and something in his knowing look told her to be strong, warning her not to give up.

I won't, she silently vowed. *Never.*

Then Gabriel lowered his head to her ear, and she heard him say, "I want you to get him ready again, Denny. Right now."

She licked her lips, remembering Jonah's taste, nearly as wonderful to her as Gabriel's, and his cock jumped, a wry smile slipping over his lips, and she smiled back, determined to bury the hurt of Gabriel's rejection.

"What about you?" she asked, sending an eager look at Gabriel over her shoulder, wanting him to take her again more than anything in the world. Well, almost anything. The only thing she wanted more was his heart...his love...his future.

"When you're around, I stay ready," he muttered, not meeting her eyes while he made such a telling admission. "Ready enough to fuck you again, angel. Right now," he growled, and she wondered if he'd read her mind.

She turned back to Jonah to find his blue eyes shining with heat...with more than mere playful desire, and she watched, transfixed, as he stroked his fingers over his thickening cock, the condom removed while she'd been looking at Gabriel, and tossed somewhere out of sight. He grabbed the washcloth from the side table, and holding her wide-eyed stare, began cleaning his beautiful shaft with long, languid strokes of the cloth, removing the taste of latex before tossing the cloth aside.

Behind her, Gabriel shifted, and then his big hands were gripping her hips, the heavy head of his cock sliding across her wet folds, and her breath caught at the heat of his flesh, even through the condom he'd slipped on without her realizing. His erection burned against her, so hot and hard and powerful—magnificent in its primal sexuality, desperate and raw lust in its most base form. He bent his knees and found her ravaged slit and began pressing, feeding himself in, a gasp breaking from her mouth at the feel of him ruthlessly forcing his way into her, the pull and burn of her swollen, tender pussy only heightening each individual sensation.

Denny gloried over every inch of his merciless penetration as she swayed forward, loving the way this man became a part of her, wanting to keep him inside of her forever.

Don't leave me, she whispered within her mind, and her heart ached with longing, even as her body burned from the soul-shattering pleasure of him entering her deeper and deeper. He forged his way inside until he was completely lodged in her core, her pussy stuffed full of him, his heavy balls jammed up snugly against her clit, and then he lowered his head to her ear. His breathing came in a ragged pattern, strained, and he rasped out in a dry voice, "Get him ready again, Denny. With my dick crammed up this hot little hole, with you squeezing me, milking me like a fist, let me watch you get him ready again."

Jonah reached up and grabbed a handful of her hair, bringing it to his nose to smell, a small, wicked smile curving the edge of his mouth. He lowered his hand, and as she bent forward, with Gabriel pushing against her back, Jonah wrapped his hand, her hair tangled with his fingers, around his cock, moving the long strands against the fat, bruised head, before shifting to stroke down the sides. He squeezed, hard, and a wet, pearly drop of fluid appeared at the crown, peering out from the nestled slit. Denny moved forward, and lapped her tongue flat across that sweet spot, licking the drop away, and he cursed roughly beneath his breath, unwinding her hair from his fist, so that she could take him back inside the wet heat of her mouth.

"Damn," he groaned as she slid over him, and Denny couldn't help but agree.

She licked him in long, strong strokes, mimicking the way she'd seen him hold himself, and then closed her mouth over the broad head and suckled, delighted when she felt the quiver quake through his hard muscles, his hips jerking, forcing him deeper. He fisted his hand around the base again, she guessed to keep himself from ramming too deep, since his hips began to thrust, pumping his cock in and out of her lips, while she lashed him with her tongue. She pulled back, breathing deeply, and he was amazingly, fully erect, oak-hard, as if he hadn't just come only moments before.

Gabriel tossed Jonah another condom, and before he'd even ripped open the seal, Gabriel's hands were positioning her legs to each side of Jonah's hips on the wide seat, while the grinning redhead shifted beneath her. And all the while, Gabriel's massive cock remained packed inside of her, locking her to him, as he braced his knees within the frame of Jonah's spread thighs, on the edge of the chair. His hands moved over her, rougher in their possession, and Denny only prayed that before the night was over, he'd find the need to never let her go.

Gabriel felt as if the top of his fucking head was about to come off as he ran his thumbs down the drenched outer lips of Denny's cunt, his cock lodged deep inside, and stroked back to the puckered, rosy entrance of her luscious ass. She shivered at his touch, and he immediately shot one wet thumb up into that tight rim of flesh before she had time to protest or object. She squealed, squirming against Jonah's long, hard body, and Gabriel pressed deeper, forcing his wet thumb up that sensitive hole before slowly pulling back. Over and over, he collected those slick, copious juices while Jonah sheathed himself in the rubber. Holding himself pressed hard and firm against the mouth of her womb, he reached out for the lube and twisted open the cap, revealing the long, tapered nozzle. His body demanded that he thrust, that he fuck, but he held himself rigid and pressed the nozzle of the lube to her puckered little hole, and squeezed, filling her tight little ass with the cool, slippery liquid.

She trembled, gasping, and Jonah said, "I'm ready, Gabe. So fucking ready."

Gabriel pulled gently from the delicious hold of her cunt, and when the other man's hands found her hips, lifting her over his dick, Gabriel moved into position.

She stiffened instantly at the feel of the thick tip prodding her sweet asshole, and he bent over her, pressing his cheek to the side of her head.

"Scared, Denny?" he whispered in her ear, taunting her.

"Don't be a bastard, Gabriel," she murmured bravely. "I told you, I'm not afraid of you."

"We'll see, angel," and he knew she could hear the smile in his voice.

"You know, Gabriel, maybe *you're* afraid of *me*?"

For a moment, he said nothing. And then, in a dark voice, he said, "Yeah, maybe I am, Denny," knowing full well it was true. It was stupid to deny it, when everyone in this room knew the truth. It was obvious what she did to him. How the hell could he hide it, with his dick sticking out hard and desperate and eager for so much as a stroke of her gaze every damn time she looked at him?

She shivered at his admission, her skin flushed with desire, excited little moans spilling past her lips, whispered and soft, making him crazed, and Gabriel felt them all the way down to the core of his cock. Felt those soft, languid sighs curl around his balls, tempting and teasing, urging him to take her, to hurtle her into the pleasure fast and hard and furious, just the way she'd demanded before — holding nothing back.

With a grunting gasp, Jonah dropped her down on his cock, jerking a sob from her throat, and Gabriel leaned forward, pressing the fat, bulging head of his dick harder to that tight, puckered entrance. He used his thumbs to spread her cheeks, knowing the tight pull would send a firestorm of pleasure around the sensitive flesh and muscles of that innocent little asshole.

"Time to see just how brave you are, angel. I want to know just how much cock you can take Denny — with Jonah packed back up inside your tiny pussy, and me reaming into this virgin little ass. And it is virgin, isn't it?" he demanded, voice guttural with all the raging hunger burning through him. "No one else has ever penetrated this tight little hole, have they, Denny? Before tonight, no one else has ever fucked it—not even with their fingers—have they?"

"N-no," she gasped, her spine going liquid beneath him as he caressed that pretty little rosebud with his cock head. "No one. Ever."

"Not any longer," he grated out of a dry throat. "This little ass belongs to me now, Denny. All mine, and I'm taking it." He pulled with his thumbs, stretching her, while pressing forward, opening that virgin entrance with the thick, heavy head of his dick, the slippery lube and her own juices helping him to force his way inside.

"*Ohmygod....ohmygod...ohmygod*," she sobbed, shaking, trembling, shivering as a violent blush of arousal raced over her fair skin, setting her on fire. Heat poured from her flesh, centered around that biting little hole that clamped down on his pulsing cock as he ruthlessly worked it into her, while Jonah did the same to her pussy, both of them shafting into her narrow, clutching passages, fighting against the mind-shattering resistance of her body.

"*It's too good...too good*," she moaned, husky voice thick with passion, and Jonah laughed, sending a rippling rumble up through his body that Gabriel felt travel through her, tremoring around the buried top inches of his dick. Denny panted, gasping for air, her body impaled by the hot, burning, throbbing mass of their cocks stuffing her so full, and he could sense the sharp-edged distress twisting there beneath the pleasure. She was in pain, but the brutal stretching of her tight, sweet little cunt and ass was smoothed by the primitive ecstasy, molded into something that she craved.

"No such thing as too good, sweet stuff," Jonah drawled, lifting his hands to tug at her nipples, a shockwave firing through her that had those vising little ass muscles clamping down so violently it made Gabriel shout. Fucking made him shout, when he wasn't even coming, while Jonah gave a wicked smile, and grunted, "No such thing at all."

Desperate to regain some sense of control, Gabriel pulled back, the thick rim of his cock head catching, dragging at her tender tissues, and Denny's head fell back on that fragile neck that drove him out of his mind. He couldn't resist sinking his teeth into that delicate line of muscle connecting her shoulder and neck, growling against her flesh at the indescribable pleasure pouring through his veins as he drove forward, pushing back through those clenching walls, plowing his cock in with another hard, driving stroke that buried him nearly halfway up that sweet, virgin backside.

"This feels so amazing," she wailed, tiny nails digging into the slick skin of Jonah's broad shoulders, making Gabriel wish he could feel their pinch against his own hungry flesh. He wanted to lay her down and cover her with the hard, heavy press of his body, imprinting each precious inch of her, branding her in every animal way as his own. Wanted her wrapped up in him until he was all that she knew, all that she smelled and tasted and felt. Until she was half as obsessed with need for him as he was with her. Until she loved him with even a fraction of the soul-tearing depth with which he *loved* her. Madly, wildly, unconditionally fucking loved her.

Oh shit. Goddamn fucking shit!

The words shouted up from his soul, screaming through the power of his blood, shaking him from head to toe, boldly refusing to be denied one single moment longer.

"Jesus—you know exactly what you fucking do to me, don't you, Denny?" he suddenly snarled, shoving another two brutally thick inches of dick up her ass, the rough blast of sound like an angry accusation growled against the wet spot on her neck where his teeth had been.

"What are you talking about?" she choked out, arching as he pressed even deeper, his head spinning with the impossibly tight feel of her ass clamping down around him, and the feel of

Jonah's hard cock ramming deeper into her pussy, rubbing against his own through the thin membrane that separated the two narrow passages with a distinct, unsettling pleasure.

Gabriel ground his forehead into that sweet spot on her neck, feeling his eyes go traitorously damp, too much breaking apart inside of him to hold any of it together.

"Why are you here, Denny? Is this all you wanted, angel? To get fucked? Why, Denny? Why are you doing this to me?" he roared, shaking, trembling from his head to his toes, everything inside of him ripped open, leaving him bleeding and raw. *"Why the fuck are you here?"*

She went still, utterly motionless against him, her back plastered to the rigid muscles of his abdomen, sweat slicking hotly between their intimately pressed flesh. "I wouldn't be here if I...if I didn't...feel *something* for you, Gabriel."

With his forehead still buried against her neck, he felt a hard, brittle laugh scrape its way out of his throat. "Yeah? And just what the hell do you feel, Denny—other than two hungry cocks shoved inside your gorgeous little body, packing you front and back? What the fuck do you feel?"

She didn't say anything, simply turned her head and looked at him with wet, tear-filled eyes over her shoulder as he lifted his face—and the look swimming there in those burnished depths gave everything away. Before he knew what he was doing, Gabriel fisted his hands in her hair, pulling her face toward his until their noses touched, breaths blasting against one another with a rapid, panting tempo.

"Why, Denny?" he demanded, eyes wild as they raced across her damp face in a desperate search for the truth. "Why are you here? Why are you giving me something like this when you don't even know me—when you don't even care a goddamn thing about me?"

He saw the flash of a decision there in her luminous gaze, then felt the gentle, loving press of her tender palm against the side of his face, as if she handed over her heart with the simple touch of her hand. He felt the rush of her feelings pour from her swollen lips, felt it pump through his body until he could feel it pounding in every cell, before she even gave him the words. "Because I do *know* you. Because I love you, Gabriel. Because I love you. That—that's why I'm here."

Choking on his breath, lungs burning, something suspiciously wet slipped down the side of his hot face as he stared at her. Oh, Christ—it was true—everything he'd ever feared about falling in love with this woman. Her lush, petal-soft mouth trembled with a smile, beautiful brown eyes wide and fragile as she stared helplessly back at him. That look ripped at him like jaws locked on his throat, demanding his surrender, and in that instant, he lost the battle. Everything snapped—control, resistance, sanity—shattering down over him like the crashing fall of the midnight sky.

His hands twisted tighter into her hair, the silken strands wound around his heavy fists, anchoring her in place as his mouth fell on hers, determined to pull everything he needed from her. It was the first time their lips had touched, after all the brutal intimacies and possessions of the night. This—*this right here*—was the first moment his tongue had breached those sexy sweet lips, plunging into the honeyed nectar of her mouth. And it was heaven, if anything so fucking raw and carnal and primal could be called such a thing.

Gabriel gasped, sobbing out snarled, masculine sounds of desperation, thrusting his tongue past her teeth, tangling it with hers, exploring the silken inner surfaces of her cheeks, the sleek enamel of her teeth. Thrilling flavors and textures that drew them together as their mouths ate at one another, savage and untamed in their need to taste everything at once. Her feminine, animal flavor swirled through his senses, washing through his blood, and pounded its way into his heart.

Everything inside—all the crap he'd struggled to keep bottled up, buried, hidden—came rushing to the surface, so hard and fast, it was like a tearing pain—as if it were all being ripped out of him, scraped from his soul. At the same time, a warm, intoxicating rush of love poured from her, filling up the open wound that had been left behind, and he felt a deep, awe-filled cry break from his throat—a feral desperation to fill her up with everything he was and had been and would ever be. To give to her all that he could be as a man and protector, and constant, devoted, ever-faithful lover.

Groaning as he pulled his hands from her hair and lowered them to her hips, Gabriel tore his mouth from hers and forced her down on Jonah's cock, hard and swift, until she'd taken him to his root, feeling the thick, rigid length surge up into her. At the same time, he thrust his way completely home, reaming into her sweet little ass until his tight balls were jammed up against Jonah's. With a roaring shout, he let the love-filled look of ecstasy washing over her tear-streaked face rip the orgasm up out of him. Hot, sizzling cum erupted from the head of his dick in a blistering, painful wave, trapped by the thin latex, his entire shaft surrounded by her clenching, grasping heat as his climax pulled both her and Jonah along with him, the three of them jerking and jolting together in a violent, primitive tangle of sweat-slicked limbs and clutching hands.

Gabriel released his savage hold on one hip to tangle his fingers back in the luxurious silk of Denny's hair, holding her steady as he ground his mouth into her own, lips and teeth smashing together, sending his wracking shouts of release tumbling down her throat, to settle possessively in her belly. They shivered and trembled, rocking together as the orgasms went on and on, draining them, a warm, bliss-filled hum left buzzing in their cells as the waves unhurriedly receded.

With his forehead pressed against hers, his lips rubbing the silken surfaces of hers, Gabriel opened his heart and gave her his soul. He fell into her as the words tumbled hoarsely from his lips, breathless and emotion-rich, so pure and true they tingled across his tongue. "I love you, Denny. God help me, angel, I'm so fucking in love with you—and I won't ever let you go."

Chapter Ten

ಬಿ

Gabriel's stunning declaration of love consumed her, thundering within Denny's veins until she knew nothing but the wondrous rush of ecstasy pouring throughout her body, pounding a rapid, bliss-filled cadence that left her trembling in his strong, solid arms. She floated dreamily within that thrumming, tender paradise, until she realized she could hear Jonah's dark chuckle under the pleasurable buzz of shocking, newfound happiness in her ears, his heavy cock still thick within the narrow walls of her sex, impaling her. The lazy sound pulled her back from the warm, sensual pool where she floated, Gabriel's harsh, yet wonderfully seductive words of love rippling around her weightless body, sheltering and possessive. With infinite care, she felt Jonah lift her hips, slipping as gently as he could from the gripping hold of her still lightly pulsing pussy.

"Hell," Jonah drawled, when he finally pulled free. Denny cast a shy peek from beneath her lashes, just in time to see a wry, wicked grin kicking up the corner of that beautiful mouth. "Talk about suddenly feeling like a third wheel."

Behind her, Gabriel snorted softly, slipping slowly from her body, his heavy arms wrapping around her middle as he smoothly pulled her to her feet. Her legs wouldn't have held her if her life had depended on it, which he seemed to understand, since he kept her glued to his front. Either that, or he simply enjoyed the pleasure of holding her close, which she desperately hoped was true. Especially since she planned on holding on to him as tightly as she could for the rest of their lives.

"Considering how this has all turned out," Gabriel sighed over her head as they stared down at the grinning man responsible for bringing them together, "I don't suppose I need to tell you thanks, or just how much I've *enjoyed* my gift." A warm edge of humor threaded through his hoarse voice — one that had never been there before — and it made Denny's heart and head go light with joy.

Jonah rolled his well-used body to its feet, lips still twisted into that wry smile as he stepped past them to snatch up his pants and boxers, while with a quiet chuckle, he peeled off the condom and, not having any other place to put it, tucked it into his pocket. After carefully working the fly closed and refastening his belt, he cut them a deep, knowing look.

"Yeah, and you don't have to tell me to hit the road, either. I know when my work is done," he added with a mischievous wink.

"Bastard," Gabriel laughed, the answering smile breaking across his face, which Denny witnessed as she twisted her head to look up at him, so brilliant, it had her grinning too.

Within seconds, Jonah had his shoes on, dark sweater pulled over his tousled auburn head, and there he stood, right before her, backlit by the flickering flames of the fire as he leaned down to place a soft, sweet kiss upon her still-damp cheek, and the warm, male scent of his skin, so much like Gabriel's, flooded her senses.

"If he ever pisses you off, sweet stuff, you know where to find me."

Gabriel squeezed her in an endearing, clutching hug, his chin resting against the top of her head. "Jonah, if I thought that was actually a possibility," he snorted, "I'd kill you, now."

"Yeah, I figured that too." And then Jonah's smile slowly faded, a serious look moving through that clear, sky-blue gaze, as he jerked his head at the man holding her so closely she could feel his heartbeat thumping rhythmically against her back. "It's good to finally see you back among the living, Gabe."

Gabriel shook his head, and Denny could all but hear the cracking edge of emotion in his gruff voice. "Hell...you're gonna make me say thank you after all, aren't you, you ass?"

That serious flash was gone in an instant, replaced by the satisfied gleam of success, if not a gentle, perhaps quiet regret. "All things considered, man, I think *I* oughta be thanking *you*." Jonah's warm, blue gaze lowered, reconnecting with her own, and he reached up to cup her jaw, rubbing the rough pad of his thumb across her lower lip. "And you, Miss Abbott— tonight was a night I know I'll never get to repeat," he laughed with a soft, rueful grin, "but one I will most definitely *never* forget. You're amazing, sweet stuff. Sexy sweet perfection from the top of your head down to those cute little toes, and I meant every word tonight. If it weren't for this ass at your back, I'd do everything I could to keep you."

A hot, brilliant blush raced over Denny's skin at his wicked words, keeping company with the low, playful growl from Gabriel vibrating against her back.

Jonah smiled at her, stroking the back of his knuckles over the furious heat in her cheeks that she couldn't disguise, then raised his gaze back to Gabriel's. "It's in your hands now, Gabe. I hope like hell you won't blow it, 'cause this is a once-in-a-lifetime chance at what every man wants." And though his tone still held that lighthearted, teasing edge from before, Denny could see the heartfelt truth beneath his words. Jonah Cartwright was a remarkable man who wanted love for himself. Who hungered for it—and yet, she could tell by the sadness he hid beneath his cavalier, playboy attitude, that he'd given up the hope of ever finding it.

With a last, lingering kiss to her lips that had Gabriel stiffening behind her, Jonah turned and let himself out, leaving them alone, and the silence of the warm, sensual wood-and-sex-scented room curled around her shoulders with a surreal air of expectation, until it was all she could do to keep from wiggling in anticipation.

A thousand emotions, worries and scenarios rapidly scrambled through her dazed mind in a chaotic jumble of *what ifs* and *what nows* — and then strong hands suddenly turned her around, and she found herself plastered against that wide, mouthwatering chest that made her long to run her greedy tongue over every hot, firm inch of masculine flesh. She dared a quick look up at gray eyes the darkening shades of a storm-kissed sky, and got caught in the smoldering striations of color, the emotion there so strong, it almost weakened her knees. A wicked, deliciously enticing smile edged up the corner of his scarred mouth, those silky, slightly swollen lips far too tempting to resist in the glow of the flickering firelight.

Denny instinctively lifted up for his kiss, needing the wondrous press of that sexy mouth against her own again, but his rough hands lifted to her face, cupping her jaw, thumbs stroking over the gentle arc of her tear-stained cheekbones.

"You love me," he whispered.

She sniffed back another telling flood of tears, undone by the simple sound of wonder in that dark voice as he said those three simple words, as if he were almost afraid to believe it was true. As if his heart was truly as vulnerable as her own. As if afraid to believe that everything it wanted stood right here for the taking.

"Figured that out, did you?" she laughed around a watery smile. "And just for the record, I've always loved you. *Always.*"

He pulled her close, the heavy length of his naked cock rubbing against her bare belly, and she wondered fleetingly what he'd done with the condom, until he laid the rough silk of his lips against her temple and said, "What Jonah did tonight — I'll never forget that he brought you to me — but it won't happen again. I can't — *won't* — share you, Denny. You're mine now. *Only* mine."

She shifted so that she could read his expression, and felt the dawning of a sweet, soft smile in her heart at the worried crease in his brow, as if she'd argue with that arrogant pronouncement. Not that she didn't plan on holding her own whenever he tried that whole dominating alpha thing with her outside of their physical relationship, but in this she was more than happy to give him her complete, unconditional surrender. Having the two of them had been a wonderful, mind-shattering, once-in-a-lifetime experience — but having Gabriel all for her own was more miraculous than anything she could have ever dreamed. "I feel the same way."

"Even though it felt good?" he teased, and Denny could have sworn those gray eyes were darkening with memories of the things she had experienced in that room — primal images that they would never repeat, but would also never forget.

She shifted, pressing closer, loving the stark look of hunger that fell over his sharp, ruggedly chiseled features as the cushion of her belly nestled closer against the brutal heat of his cock, her tight nipples smashed against the muscular slabs of his chest.

"*You* feel good."

"Are you sure this is what you want, Denny?" he asked in a suddenly hard voice, as if the rough tone could mask the unfamiliar thread of vulnerability revealed by his question, while demanding she answer truthfully — proving that he still couldn't believe the hand that fortune had dealt him here tonight.

"I love you, Gabriel. Of course this is my choice."

"You came to me and offered yourself," he rasped in a throaty, growling whisper, grasping her shoulders, "and I'm keeping you, Denny. Claiming you, and you'll have to kill me before I'll ever let you go."

Trying to soothe the fierce, red-tinged energy she could feel pulsing off his body, all animal maleness and dominance at its most elemental, she cupped his hot face in her palms, feathering the heated, stubble-shadowed flesh with her fingertips.

"Considering I only ever want to be in your arms, I don't think you're in any mortal danger." She smiled softly, lowering her hands to grasp onto his bulging biceps, squeezing and stroking the firm, round muscles beneath her touch. Then she leaned forward and rubbed her lips over his collarbone, thrilling at the masculine taste and scent of his sleek, fever-warm skin.

His long, deft fingers moved into her hair, sifting through the long strands, studying how the firelight danced over it with a tender, greed-filled look that charmed her all the way down to her toes, a boyish hope beginning to kindle there in that stormy gaze. "And if Jonah ever so much as shakes your hand, I'm breaking his fucking fingers."

"Now, Gabriel, you don't sound very grateful," she teased, raising up on her tiptoes to lick a provocative circle around the base of his throat that had his impressive cock jerking against her in a mouthwatering display of carnal need, every muscle in that tall, sculpted body going hard with scorching, emotional lust. "And after all he did for you…"

"I'm afraid my appreciation only goes so far," he rumbled with that crooked grin that pulled at her heart. Lifting her into his arms, he ignored her squealing protest as he carried her through the archway leading into his moonlit bedroom, not stopping until he'd reached a bathroom she could have sworn was the size of her entire apartment. "I'm finding that where you're concerned, I'm as possessive as they come, angel."

Denny smiled with a rich, warm rush of womanly delight, rubbing her fingers through the short, silky scruff of his dark hair—so black it gleamed like ink in the gentle shadows of the night. "You're not the only possessive one here, Gabriel."

For a moment, his arms simply tightened around her, squeezing the breath from her lungs, and then he said, "Good—that's what I was counting on."

A small laugh played in his throat, more evidence of his happiness with her admission, while he flicked a panel on the wall, and the spacious room immediately filled with a soft, soothing light. She couldn't help but blink against the warm, inviting perfection of sand-colored marble, beveled mirrors and thick, sage-colored bath rugs, as he carried her to a decadent, marbled combination Jacuzzi bath and enclosed shower. Settling her gently on her feet within the crook of his arm, Gabriel reached in with the other and twisted a series of knobs that had a hot, misting flow of water surging from no less than six gleaming showerheads. Denny figured she must have looked as stunned as she felt, because he gave a deep, rough rumble of laughter as he lifted her into the marble tub with him, holding her against the erotic heat of his body as the water sprayed against her sore, aching muscles, pulling a low moan from her throat that she couldn't hold inside.

"Feel good?" he asked, staring down at her, mesmerizing her with the masculine beauty of his mist-covered face and that sinful, outrageously beautiful body that spoke of sheer male animal strength, predatory and powerful. Glistening drops of water clung to the long, ink-black lashes framing those seductive eyes, the gray depths shot with silver, smoldering with not only a physical, but a gripping emotional hunger that she longed to satisfy in every way. Large hands settled onto her shoulders, easing the knotted muscles with a gentle yet firm massage, slowly working their way down her spine, pulling her closer into the primal heat and hardness of his length. "We worked you hard tonight, didn't we, angel?"

Denny licked her lips, afraid to say the words, but knowing that she couldn't hold them inside. "Gabriel, tonight, this—everything," she stumbled. "It's not going to ever cause problems for us, is it?"

He pulled her closer, so tall and strong and wide, and yet she felt utterly protected, as if sheltered beneath his protective wing, knowing that he'd die to keep her safe. "He may have touched your body, Denny, but I was the only one touching your heart. Do you know what I saw in that room tonight?"

She shook her head, a whispery, "No," falling from her trembling lips, the warm steam of the shower filling her lungs, making her drowsy with a heavy, smoothly flowing wave of relaxation.

"I saw a breathtakingly beautiful, impossibly brave woman willing to step into territory she'd never traveled before, hoping it would lead her to a way to break through to me. And it did, Denny. Jonah knows me too well not to have known all along what having you under me would do."

She blinked up at him in the mist-thickened air, face damp with a mixture of water and tears as love and hope drummed furiously through her veins. "And what do you see now?"

"I see *you. My Denny,*" he growled. "Honest and real and so impossibly fucking perfect, it blows my mind, not to mention my cock. Just looking at you makes me ache, angel. Just looking at these lips, this hair." His eyes caressed each misted feature, while his powerful hands trailed down her sides, navigating the abundant curves she'd always hated, but for the first time in her life, began to see through the love-filled eyes of a man. *Her man.*

He smiled at her, a wicked, outrageously seductive smile, and grabbed onto her fingers, lifting them to her breasts, molding them to her flesh with his big, strong hands, his eyes glittering in the warm mist. "Hold these gorgeous tits for me, angel, while I taste them again."

Her cheeks burned as he positioned her hands where he wanted them, so that she was offering her breasts up like plentiful melons, and he saw the strange rush of shyness that flooded through her, just like he saw everything.

"Please," he rasped, still smiling, those beautiful gray eyes pleading. "You're so beautiful, Denny. Just like this, with your skin misty and the water falling over you like rain. Please," he groaned, lowering his head to capture one sensitive nipple between his teeth. "You're so damn sweet, it fucking kills me. Drives me outta my mind."

He suckled her, strong jaws working as he ravaged her nipple with lips and tongue, gently tugging, until her legs were pressing together, trying to ease the renewed ache thrumming through her clit, clenching her inner muscles.

With wide eyes, she watched him smile around her nipple, lashing it with his clever tongue, while one big hand moved back between her thighs, two thick fingers pressing deeply into the aching heat of her pussy, making her back arch, forcing her nipple further into his mouth. He closed his lips and with the flat of his tongue, pressed the sensitive peak against the roof of his mouth, sucking hard, while rubbing it with that wicked tongue, and Denny could have sworn she saw spots swimming before her eyes, glittering and black, as infinite as space.

"*Gabriel,*" she cried out, her voice husky and raw, and the sound of his name on her lips must have sent him over the edge, because he ripped his mouth away from her breast with a guttural growl, only to lift up and fist his free hand into her hair, gripping the back of her skull as he took her mouth with a brutal, savage hunger that had her lips mashed into her teeth, his tongue plunging and invading with savage skill. She sobbed into his mouth as he ravaged her, consumed her, undone by his violent passion, and felt his fingers slip from her body. He pulled back, and raised them to her mouth, painting her lips with the warm, musky scent of her juices, his gray eyes dark and wild, filled with primitive hunger that seemed to pulse off of his big, hard body in dizzying, electrifying waves, surrounding her.

"So fucking sweet, angel," he moaned in a low, aching tone, then lowered his head and swiped his tongue across her lips, eating at her juice-covered mouth with slow, tortuous strokes that she knew were meant to drive her mad.

"Gabriel, please," she panted, ready to beg, the heavy, churning ache between her legs so intense, she would have thrown him to the floor of the shower and had her wicked way with him, if she'd possessed the strength. But she was wrecked, barely able to stand, deliciously assaulted by the heavy, pulsing pleasure he so easily pressed upon her.

"Do you know what these curves of yours do to me, Denny?" he muttered, pulling slightly away from her body, his deep voice distracted by his slow, intent study of her as he took her hands from her breasts and lifted them high above her head, forcing her to her toes as he stretched her out. "How fucking hard and hot they make me? All of you, every inch of this gorgeous, fucking unbelievable little body makes me think about wrapping myself around you and holding on forever. For always."

The steam clung to his thick black lashes, the gray warming from the sensual heat until his eyes roiled with the flickering silvery flames, like bubbling mercury. "So smooth," he rasped. "Like soft, slippery satin." He secured her wrists in one hand, while the other moved over her, rough in its possession, the primitive need she could feel trembling through its touch setting a raging wave of want thundering through her blood.

"You'd think I'd promise to be gentle with you," he gritted through his teeth, jaw held so tightly that she saw the muscles tic at one side. He wrapped his arm around her waist and lifted her, walking her into the back wall of the shower, trapping her there with the hot, heavy press of his body against hers, her toes not even touching the luxurious marble beneath her feet. "But I won't be gentle with you, angel. I *can't.* We—you and I—no way in hell are we finished tonight. I could ride you from now 'til sunrise, and it still wouldn't be enough.

"This is gonna take some time," he rasped in that hard, guttural voice, setting her on her feet and releasing her wrists as he reached to a corner shelf and grabbed an amber-colored bottle of soap, pouring the crisp, rich fragrance into his hands before working them over her sensitive skin, cleaning her from head to toe. And all the while, that deep, dark voice captivated her. "A few days of nothing but learning your gorgeous little body inside and out, and then, just maybe by then I'll be able to let you out of bed. We can drop by the office, collect your things until we figure out what you want to do—but I don't want you slaving away there day after day when you belong with me, by my side. And we'll need to make arrangements to have your apartment packed up, have everything moved over here.

"We're gonna be busy as hell, and it won't be easy, Denny, because all I'm going to want to do is drag your sexy little ass right back to bed. Morning, day, and night. Take you back to bed and fuck you until you can't remember your name. Until you can't remember anything but that you belong to me. And you'll take it. You'll take my cock, each and every time I feed it into your hungry little cunt. You'll take it because it's yours. No one else's. It's never belonged to anyone like this, and it never will again. Only you, angel. *Only you.*"

She swallowed, lungs tight, knowing that she'd have arguments later, at least when it came to her job. But for now she was simply too stunned to give voice to any of the words tangling wildly in her mind, the beautiful, intense emotion burning there in his glittering, storm-dark eyes melting into her, making her feel as pliant as soft, melted caramel, ready to be molded beneath his masterful, dominant hands.

The feel of his power, of his raw-edged masculine energy and animal strength, intoxicated her—the need with which he looked at her, hitting her like a drug within her system. The warm, tactile heat of his hair-roughened limbs, the sleek, silky skin of his chest, the solid, mouthwatering muscles buried beneath all that firm flesh, the sheer weight and dominance of his body against her own—all of it pulled her under his seductive spell, pulling him even deeper into her heart.

And that cock. That massive, powerful, mesmerizing cock. She loved its thick ridges of veins—how they pulsed with the heavy throb of blood beneath the hot, silky skin. Loved how it flexed and jerked, alive with primitive hunger.

She wanted to study it forever. Wanted to catalog taste and texture, scent and sensitivity.

He moved back, and strong hands held her shoulders, pulling her forward, then turning her beneath the pulsing spray of the shower heads until the fresh-scented bubbles had been washed away and she stood before him wearing nothing but her pink, rosy skin, hair hanging around her shoulders in long, sopping ropes. Her teeth bit into her lower lip, vulnerable feelings of insecurity working their way back into her mind as she stood before such blatantly male perfection. But then he nudged that thick, glorious cock, so impossibly hard and drumming with need, into her soft belly, and she forgot about being too plump or round or plain. With an avid hunger, she longed to drag her tongue down his hard abdomen, following the meandering trails of water, until she found that fat, bruised cock head and sucked it eagerly between her lips. Sucked and licked and ate at it until it exploded into her mouth and his hot, blistering cum flooded down her throat, filling her with a part of him that was *all hers*.

A flare of scorching heat blazed through his gaze, as if he'd read her thoughts right there on her flushed face, and everything became a blur of movement and rough, soughing breath. The water stopped, the air still thick with steam while warm, plush towels moved over her body and hair, drying her. Hands clutched and gripped, her body weightless once more as he carried her into his bedroom, and Denny found herself tossed into the middle of a sprawling, silk-covered bed, Gabriel's dark head buried between her sprawled thighs before she'd even finished bouncing.

The golden light from the bathroom stole into the moonlit room like a fog, soft and low, allowing her eyes to seek out the seductive heat of his expression as he stared at her sex, stroking the swollen folds with the rasping pads of his fingers. He gathered up her slippery cream, the long digits sticky and wet as they found his lips and he sucked them into his mouth, his tongue working around each finger, eating her flavor, moaning at the pure, evocative taste of her lust.

"You're so damn sweet, Denny."

He studied her while he snagged a condom from the pile he'd left on the corner of the bed, rolling the thin latex over his heavy cock, gray eyes intent, focused solely on her pulsing flesh as it throbbed with slick, insistent need. Her juices flowed warm and free, thick with want, and that wicked smile curled once more at the edge of his bad boy mouth, making her wild with the desire to bite and lick, ravish and devour.

"Do you like being eaten out?" he whispered, stroking her, every touch of his fingers an act of ownership, of possession, pulling low, husky moans from her throat with the ease of a maestro. "Do you, beautiful? I sure as hell hope so, because I'm going to be giving you head as often as you can take it, angel. Make meals out of you. Drag you into my office, spread your legs as you lie back on my desk, and eat this ripe, drenched little pussy for lunch. Suck and lick and tongue-fuck you until you can feel the pleasure pumping in every cell of this sexy-as-sin body, going and going until you give me what I want. Until you ripple and scream and gush against my face. Until I can feel your sweet, sticky cum filling my mouth, and then I'll just eat you deeper, demanding you give me every fucking little drop.

"And only when you've given me everything, only then will you get *this*," he growled, moving over her, pressing her knees up high and wide with his strong hands. "Just not this time, Denny. Not tonight. Christ, tonight I can't fucking wait. I have to be in you, now," he growled, nearly shouting, punctuating his promise with a thick, cramming thrust of his hips. His own knees dug into the mattress and his brutal cock hit her hard and high, pushing a rough sob up out of her throat, shoving through her tight walls with a savage determination that made her scream. He shafted into her, beyond mercy as he penetrated her with each thick, throbbing inch of his cock, working his way into her until she'd taken him to his balls. Then he trembled, muscles quaking as the fat width of his cock head lodged against the mouth of her womb, and he held himself deep, giving her straining, panicked, tender vaginal muscles the time to adjust.

"But after tonight, I'm going to love making you wait for the ride, sweetheart," he groaned, voice guttural and hoarse, muscles tremoring with the need to move…to hammer himself into her. "I'll always give you as much cock as you can take, Denny, but not until you give me what I want first. Not until you give me *this*." He released her knees and braced himself on one powerful arm as he slipped the questing fingers of his other hand through her folds, drenching them with her juices as he rimmed the aching place where he stretched her so wide. Then he raised his hand and rubbed the slick, pearly fluid over her trembling lips, just like he'd done in the shower.

He leaned over her, his smile wolfish and sure, as dangerous as it was sexy, and held her wide-eyed gaze as his tongue slipped out of his mouth and he lapped at her lower lip, moaning, while her cunt clutched at him like a squeezing, pumping fist. "So sweet, Denny. So fucking sweet, I can't believe you're real—that you're mine."

And then he moved, his heavy cock head catching at her raw, scalding tissues, and the beauty of his possession nearly made her scream with triumph. Her legs were spread around his powerful hips, her pussy open and glistening, sopping with the sweet musk of her juices, impaled by Gabriel's thick, raging cock. She lifted her head to watch as it penetrated her, stretching the mouth of her vagina so impossibly wide, the surrounding skin crimson and quivering, his ruddy, heavy-headed dick reaming into her over and over, each thrust and withdrawal sending icy-hot shards of bliss through her system. She could hardly breathe, hardly take in all the sensory overload—unable to understand how someone so breathtakingly magnificent could take so much pleasure from her plain, plump body.

But he did. She could see it in the tight strain of his features, the taut bunch of his muscles, and the pleasure-glazed look in those silver-flecked eyes. He was *making love* to her, and he loved it—honestly *loved* it—and the pride that knowledge sent through her was as overwhelming as the pleasure he pumped into her quivering flesh with each pounding, hammering stroke. His tempo held complete and utter purpose, every flex and thrust forged with the determination to make her crazy, to drive her out of her mind—and it was working.

He ripped her deeper into that warm, swirling pool of pleasure, all the intimate details of his body imprinted into her brain, inscribed upon her senses. The sensual feel of his skin slapping against her own—its taste and silk-rough textures like a sensual dreamscape where each and every one of her fantasies found life. The unending stretching, so painful as that broad, drumming head crammed its way deeper into her body, wide shaft separating her tender tissues, and the even thicker root pulling her vulva unbearably open. It would have been too much—far too much—were it not for the slick, slippery juices coating her inner walls, slipping wetly from the tiny mouth of her pussy as he thrust that massive cock in and out of the tight, tender hole. His muscles bunched and flexed, sweat flying from their fevered bodies as he worked her harder and harder, packing her full, forcing the pleasure into her until it all blended together into one endless penetration of ecstasy. His weight and the smell of his skin. The raw, keening cries of joy as they ripped from her throat and his low, guttural groans. The sensual, slapping echoes of rigid flesh moving within wet, clinging tissues.

"That's it, Denny," he growled, savage and wild in his need as his hips powered between her wide spread thighs, brutally pumping his massive cock into her tight, clenching depths, cramming him in deeper and deeper. "Come for me again, angel. Let me feel it. I want your tight little cunt sucking on my dick," he groaned, burying his face in her neck, his lips and teeth moving against her skin while he gave her the most violent, mind-shattering ride she could have ever imagined. "Now, angel. *Right now.*"

It was like an explosion, all infinite blackness and blinding, showering sparks of silvery light as they fell into the ravaging pleasure together, lost in the potent, sensual storm of love and lust as their hoarse shouts filled the air—and they must have collapsed into sleep, because the moon burned higher in the endless sky beyond the amber glass of the tall windows when she next opened her eyes to the feel of Gabriel kissing his way down her tingling body, his cock already sheathed in a new condom.

A rumbling growl came from between her legs, and she felt its vibration shimmying through the sensitive cushion of her pussy, up the tight channel of flesh, quickening like a flood over and through her skin until peaking in her nipples, her temples thrumming with the sudden burst of sensation. She felt tight and full, as if her skin had shrunk too small for the pleasures filling it—any moment expecting it to beam out through her pores like fiery shafts of light, piercing and bright, a pumping glow of lust-colored bliss.

His head rose slowly from between her legs, mouth and chin wet with her juices, eyes so intense they mirrored the storm-clouded horizon at the height of a hurricane. Roiling, flickering flames of gray, seeing straight down to the raw, twisting emotions seeking comfort within her heart. "Are you mine?"

He didn't growl the question. Didn't command. It was simply stated, the choice hers as to what she gave back—he gave no order, no demand. He asked for what he wanted, and she was helpless to deny him. Helpless to deny herself. Why should she, when their aims and goals were the same? *Closer. More. Everything.*

"I'm yours," Denny said, her voice like smoke, ethereal and softly fleeting, as if she were unable to draw enough air into her lungs. "Are you mine?"

"Forever, angel." His eyes closed, throat working as he swallowed hard and moved over her, slowly pressing his body against her own, as if savoring every moment, each individual point of contact. Beautiful, taut lines of emotion flowed over his magnificent length, borne forth from his soul, making him shiver with a weakness that touched her in a way no act of dominance ever could. He braced his weight on his forearms and lifted his face—smoldering, intense, storm-ridden eyes catching her, trapping her—and she watched his words emerge from that scarred mouth as if in a trance, mesmerized by the beauty and raw emotion of the intimate, breathtaking moment as he pushed back inside of her, so solid and strong. "Christ, Denny, I've *never* felt like this."

"Me either," she whispered with another watery smile, her spine arching beneath him as he pressed closer, the heavy beat of his heart thrumming against her own.

"Do you know what you do to me?" he rasped, voice aching with emotion as he stared into her eyes. "I don't think I lived until tonight, Denny. I don't think I've ever really been alive until you opened my heart. Do you have any idea how much I love you? I'd tell you, but I don't even know how to put it into words—all I can do is show you."

And he did. He rode her body, giving her the succulent, sumptuous pleasure of ecstasy over and over, until she was writhing beneath his provocative rhythm and the feel of his body throbbing inside of her, pulse beating to the pumping of his blood in that thick, thrusting shaft. It went on and on, until the pleasure claimed them again and they trembled over the mind-shattering edge, surrendering to the thundering ecstasy, clinging to one another through the violent storm. They clung and shivered and held, soaked in the rich, intimate spill of the other's scent and taste, limbs tangled in a carnal knot meant to tie them closer...and closer...as the stars climbed higher beyond the tall windows and heartbeats slowed, finding a meaningful rhythm of one.

And in the quiet, shadowed intimacy of the night, Denny placed her hand over his heart and said, "Tell me about the scars, Gabriel."

The tightening along the length of his body was subtle, but still enough for her to notice, considering she was plastered to him from shoulder to ankle—and yet he didn't deny her. He simply said, "I figured Jonah already told you all there was to know, Denny. You sure you want me to rehash it?"

"He told me a little. That you got in trouble a lot for fighting. That you had a girlfriend in college and that she died. Some kind of tragic misunderstanding that you blamed yourself for."

"That's about it," he sighed, voice gruff as he rolled over onto his back, pulling away from her.

"Tell me, Gabe."

"Why? So you can know how much of a bastard I am?"

She searched to find his expression in the soft, glowing shaft of light streaming in from the bathroom, needing to see the look in those gray eyes that opened into his soul.

"No, so you can trust me to understand. Trust me enough to share the truth. To share your life, the good and the bad. No one is perfect. Not even you, Mr. Almighty Harrison."

In the shimmering shaft of light, she watched that wicked mouth curl up at the corner. "You're impertinent, you know that, angel?"

"You said I was real—and I want to know all about the 'real' you, past and present. I'm also the woman in love with you, body and heart and soul. I deserve to know everything about you. To understand your demons, no matter how ugly or hurtful they are."

"It isn't pretty," he muttered, staring up at the ceiling, one arm braced beneath his dark head, profile ruggedly handsome in the soft, amber light washing over his closed expression.

Denny braced herself on her elbow, stroking the warm skin over his heart, reminding him that her love would be there, no matter what horrors he held inside. "Real life isn't always pretty."

He swallowed, throat working, and with the sound of gravel in his throat, he finally said, "I left her."

She nodded, not understanding, but knowing that he needed to say this in his own way. "You broke up with her?"

"No—I *left* her, at the bar, with the bastard who killed her. I put my ass in my truck and drove away, and left her there to die."

"What happened?" she asked softly, gently.

His voice took on the emotionless monotone of one who didn't care, but Denny knew it was only because he cared too much. He kept the pain locked deep within, where it festered, raw and unforgiving. Gabriel hadn't forgiven himself, and until he did, those wounds would continue to rip him apart inside, bleeding him dry.

But he wasn't alone any longer—and because she loved him, Denny longed to help him heal.

Chapter Eleven

ဢ

In that gentle blanket of darkness, Denny pressed warm and soft at his side, Gabriel heard himself tell the story that had changed him from the rowdy, live-life-to-its-fullest boy he'd been, to the cold-hearted bastard he'd become, hiding behind those numbing walls of ice. He told her of how he'd met Karen during his senior year at college, and how they'd dated for the better part of the year, though he hadn't realized she'd taken their relationship quite so seriously, until it was too late.

And then he told her about the Friday night when Karen insisted they ditch a party at Jonah's apartment, and go see some local band instead. He told her about how the club was a dive, and how from the moment they'd arrived, Karen, flanked by several of her sorority sisters, had set out to make him jealous, flirting with an older group of guys.

"We're getting the hell out of here," he'd argued, but she wouldn't leave, and so he'd sat there through two shitty bands, watching her and her friends dance their way through that low-life, rough-looking group. Already in trouble with the University for fighting, he'd known he'd be expelled if he got caught in another confrontation, no matter where it took place. And so he'd watched, refusing to take the bait she'd seemed to be testing him with, and it had pissed her off, his lack of response to the fact that other men flirted with her. Her looks had begun to take on an angry, resentful edge.

"I thought you loved me," she'd sneered, pale face flushed dark with color as her lip had curled and she'd spat venom at him. "But you don't care a goddamn thing about what I do, do you, Gabe? All you care about is yourself." Then she'd headed to the ladies room with her friends, casting him one last, furious glare, and he'd decided that when she came back, he was dragging her ass home, whether she fought him or not.

But she hadn't come back. When her friends returned without her, he'd walked over to ask one of them where she'd gone. She'd answered him with a shrug and a blank look.

And then he'd noticed part of that group of guys at the back entrance of the bar, crowded around the open door, as if guarding it, and a sick feeling had twisted his gut, tearing inside of him, ugly and raw. He'd tried to shoulder his way past them, and all hell had broken loose. Two of them had knives.

He'd been so stunned when the first blade came at him, he'd jumped back then reached for the bastard's wrist. He'd broken the guy's bones in one fist and crushed his face with the other. Chaos erupted as one of them swung a chair at his bad knee, while the other slashed at his face.

In a blind rage, he'd finally worked his way through two more of the dickheads, while some of the band members pulled the others off, and limped his way through the back door. And there she'd been, jeans around her slim ankles while the asshole she'd been flirting with all night fucked her upside the dingy, outside wall, her head thrown back, a glazed look of strange serenity falling over those delicate features, arms looped trustingly around the bastard's shoulders. A staggering sense of betrayal had torn through him, because she'd looked as if she'd wanted to be right there, with that stranger pounding into her.

Clearing his throat, eyes hot with emotion, Gabriel finished his story. "She wasn't fighting him, wasn't struggling, and in that moment, all I could think about through the haze of pain and fury clouding my mind was getting away. I drove myself to the ER, took a cast on my knee after emergency surgery, ten stitches for the cut on my face and more in my arm.

"I didn't trust myself—what I'd do to her—so I left, Denny. I left her there, thinking she was just a bitch getting screwed because that's what she wanted, figuring one of her friends could take her home when she was through with him.

"Only, she never made it home. He killed her. They found her strangled, naked, in a ditch ten miles from that fucking seedy little trap, her blood pumped full of some kind of date rape shit he'd been slowly slipping into her drinks. He didn't even try to hide the evidence, he'd been so strung out on God only knows what. A bit of everything, the cops said."

"Oh God," Denny whispered, moving closer to his side, giving comfort with the simple touch of her skin against his own.

The hand on his abdomen balled into a fist, the old pain and guilt ripping through him, staggering in its intensity. "And I should've fucking known. If I hadn't been so stupidly angry at her for pulling her little stunt, I'd have paid more attention to how she was acting, that glazed look in her eyes and violent color in her face. But I was too busy trying to control my temper, covering my own ass, just like she said.

"And later on, her friends told me that her parents had been riding her hard about us getting married. She was afraid to tell me, and she thought making me jealous that night would move up the proposal she'd been so sure was coming. Bring me to heel and all that crap. That had been her plan for going there all along, if you can believe it. And you know what the really sad part is? I hadn't even been thinking about proposing to her. It'd never even crossed my mind. I cared about her, but I didn't love her. Not like I love you. And she died because of that."

"No, that's not why she died," Denny murmured, swallowing thickly. "Her death was tragic, but it wasn't your fault. How were you supposed to know that she wasn't there with him by choice? Your reaction was natural, Gabriel. Better than what some men would have done, taking their anger out on her with their fists. You didn't kill her, those monsters did. I know it must be hard to accept, but it was their sin—not yours."

"Yeah, well, I didn't save her either."

"No, you didn't. And you have to forgive yourself for that. You couldn't have known, not given the circumstances of that night, and I know you were hurting, both physically and emotionally. You're human, whether you want to believe it or not. Magnificent, yes, but human all the same. You can't read minds and tell the future. You know, you have to forgive yourself for being just a man."

"It's not that simple."

"Isn't it?" she asked softly, stroking that fragile hand over his heart, his love for her burning within that vulnerable organ like a brilliant, blazing flame, heating him from the inside out.

"Hell, I don't know," he rasped, blowing out a hard breath, wanting to believe her, but knowing it was going to take time.

"Then it's a good thing I do," she murmured with another one of those soft, warm smiles that he could feel melting into him. "I know all about being just an average, poking along little human."

Gabriel cut her a hard, glittering glare. "There's not a goddamn average thing about you, woman. And it pisses me off to hear you say it."

"Then I guess we'll have to work on these flaws together. I know it will take time, but I'll be here for you, always. Whadya say, Mr. Harrison?"

Turning on his side, he laid his head on the soft down of the pillow, staring at the gentle, beautiful face of the woman who held his heart and always would. "I say that I love you, Denny."

And it was true. He loved her more than any man could love a woman—loved her as part of his heart, of his soul, that he couldn't live without. He wasn't healed, but he would be. Someday. With her love and warmth, he had a brilliant hope for the promise of their future, with Denny by his side, loving him, filling his life with happiness and helping him come to an understanding and acceptance of his past mistakes. Helping him to forgive himself.

He loved her, and damn it, he finally felt as if it might not be a sin to accept the love that she offered in return. Sin or not, he had no choice. To give her up would be like giving up air or water. She'd become a vital necessity for existence, and without her, that numbing cold he'd carried for so long would invade his chest, freezing off his heart, until the tortured organ no longer held a beat within its rhythm.

"Do you understand what that means?" he asked, capturing her hand, squeezing her fingers, bringing them to his lips. "How much I care about you? What I'd do for you?"

He shifted onto an elbow, urging her to her back with a hand on her chest, over the rapid pounding of her heart, then laid her hair out over the pillow, spreading and separating the silken strands, marveling over the refreshing, natural beauty of her makeup free face and soft, creamy skin in the pale shafts of light.

"I'll be yours, Denny, forever. Faithful. Honest. I know I'll make mistakes and that I can be a real bastard when the mood strikes, but I'll never cheat and I'll never wander. And when I'm a grouch, I expect you to be here to kick my ass into shape."

A wanton smiled curled across that lush, pink mouth that he loved, tempting him to lose himself in its voluptuous textures and tastes. "I can handle that. Do I get to kick it into bed?"

"God," he muttered, nibbling on her lower lip, unable to control the feral hunger for her that thundered through his blood. Not even wanting to. "I think you'll be lucky if you can ever get me out of bed, woman."

Lifting his face, Gabriel stared down at her, his eyes hot and damp, lost in the searing emotion of the night. "You love me," he whispered in a sound of awe, jaw tight with love and lust and the thick, drugging pleasure of having her in his arms.

She glowed with life, wispy strands of hair caught on her damp, flushed cheeks, eyes luminous and heavy-lidded while her lips remained parted for her gently rushing breath. "Yes," she whispered, "I love you."

"You're going to marry me," he rasped against the silken heaven of her mouth as he lowered his face to hers, tasting her with his tongue as he pulled her beneath him, wanting to stay there — *right there* — forever.

When he raised his head, her lips curved in a slow, bliss-filled smile that trailed down his spine with licking pleasure. "Mmm...we're going to marry each other."

"I own you," he growled, pumping his hips against the gentle cushion of her warm, wet pussy as she eagerly parted her thighs, but not yet entering her, torturing them both.

She blinked, dark lashes casting deep shadows over the smooth perfection of her cheeks, and nodded her head in ready agreement. "That too — I've belonged to you since the moment you first looked at me, Gabriel."

"You own me too, Denny. Body, heart, and soul, just like you said."

"Mmm...and I'll be keeping you," she moaned, arching beneath him, all that creamy, sensuous skin flushed with desire, gleaming like pale, pink satin. He shifted, moving to claim the swollen silk of her lips again, when she suddenly said, "Wait—"

He searched her eyes, wondering why she stopped him, the melting, taffy-soft folds of her sweet little cunt pulsing against the hard, desperate length of his cock. "What?"

"Thank you." She brushed her fingers through the short scrub of his hair, let her index finger trail down his high forehead, following the slightly crooked line of his nose, over his rough upper lip, stroking his scar, until it trailed sweetly over his chin, down his throat, and landed against the thundering beat of his heart. "With all my heart, Gabriel. Thank you for trusting me."

"Don't thank me, Denny. I love you. How could I not trust you, angel?"

She smiled at him, smoothing one black brow, then sweeping her finger across his lower lip, laughing as he playfully tried to nip the slender digit. "What were you going to say, that day in the hallway when you stole my lunch?"

His cheeks went warm with color, but he knew she wouldn't let him charm his way out of answering. "Come on, big guy," she said with a saucy grin, "'fess up."

"I was only going to speak the truth."

She smiled expectantly. "Which was?"

"Mine," he murmured, lips already returning her playful grin. "I was going to say that you're *mine*."

He watched her gaze soften, knew he was looking at her like a lovesick sap, loving that she was looking at him the same way. "I think I probably would have fainted at your feet," she sighed, her grin becoming a sultry smile. "Or thrown you to the ground and had my wicked way with you."

"Anytime, angel. You're the only woman who will ever be having her wicked way with me ever again, and I'm expecting you to take full advantage of the opportunities on a constant basis."

"Ya know, I think maybe you're a sex addict," she teased playfully, pulling her bottom lip through her teeth, the seductive action making his eyes darken with hunger. "Lucky me."

"I'm a Denny addict. And proud to admit it. Almost as proud as I am to admit how much I love you," he groaned, covering her with the hot, solid, heavy weight of his body, wrapping her close in the unbreakable hold of his arms. "I don't think I'll ever be able to say it enough times."

"I'll never be able to hear it enough," she moaned. "But just so you know, I love you...*more*."

He grunted his disagreement, mumbling the words into her delicate flesh as his mouth trailed moist, biting kisses down her throat, across the smooth skin of her chest, moving from one tender nipple to the other, causing her to arch in pleasure. "Not possible."

"Hmm…we'll see."

Gabriel lifted his face, one black brow arched in laughing humor. "Is that another dare?"

"And if it is, what are you going to do about it?"

He moved one hot, damp palm down to cup her bottom. "Spank this gorgeous ass until it burns a bright, glowing shade of pink to match those pretty blushing cheeks."

She shivered, and a slow, sexy sweet smile curled across her lush mouth as she rolled her hips, making him shake with the pulsing heat of her soft, drenched pussy kissing his hard belly. "You know what I say to that, birthday boy?"

"What?" Gabriel gasped, wondering if she'd soon push him to the point where he begged her to let him take her again, right now, hard and fast and violently, fucking her through the damn mattress until they both exploded.

Pressing that luscious smile to his tingling lips, she breathed the wicked words into him, burning him with the pleasure of everything that she was, feeling as if he'd burst from the satisfaction of knowing that it would always be *his*.

"Say it again, angel," he rasped, nipping at her lip, utterly lost in her. "Say it again."

Denny pulled away, the teasing delight in the burnished depths of her eyes promising him a lifetime of mind-shattering passion and love, as she licked that plump bottom lip and whispered those three little words that had stolen his heart.

"I *dare* ya."

Epilogue
One Month Later

&

Gabriel rounded the corner, turned down the corridor on his left, and headed toward the wing that held his, Jonah's, and Lucas' private offices. A shit-eating grin curved the edges of his mouth as he envisioned Denny's reaction to the gift he carried in his briefcase, its leather handle gripped securely in his right hand, while a lavish bouquet of orchids and jasmine—their sweet scent ripe and wild, fragile ivory petals dew-kissed and satin-soft—filled his left. The flowers were for now, but the gift was for tonight, and he couldn't wait to show it to her.

And then use it on her, he thought with a wicked chuckle.

His cock stood up to attention at the erotic, wildly arousing images flooding his mind, and he gave a wry shake of his dark head as he took a deep breath and tried to cool himself down. Damn thing seemed to think he was sixteen again, and he had a warm feeling that with Denny by his side, for the rest of his life, it always would.

A door opened just ahead of him, and Jonah stepped into the sunlit corridor, the line of his lips tight with strain until he caught sight of the flowers and Gabriel's unmistakably warm expression. Then the corner of his wide mouth kicked up into a knowing grin and his blue eyes shone with satisfaction.

"Oh man," Jonah laughed, clasping him on the shoulder as he leaned over and took a dramatic whiff of the sweet-smelling, satin-wrapped bouquet. "I take it that your proposal was met with a favorable response last night, eh?"

"Did you have any doubts as to my powers of persuasion?" he drawled, lifting his brows.

"Never a one," Jonah replied, returning a smile that Gabriel knew was genuine, despite his feelings for Denny. Feelings he knew Jonah had walked away from after that one unforgettable night. But Jonah had remained nothing but honorable and honest, as steadfast a friend as Gabriel had ever known, and he knew that the guy genuinely wished him well.

"Did you do it proper?" Jonah asked, rocking back on his heels, dark auburn brows lifted in taunting inquiry.

"Down on one knee and everything," Gabriel chuckled, recalling with hot satisfaction how Denny had stared down at him after they'd come in from dinner, and he'd knelt before her. Her eyes had been wide and tear-damp, her gaze liquid and infinitely tender as he'd pulled the black satin jeweler's box from his pocket. When he'd flipped open the top, she'd gasped, covering her trembling mouth with her hand, looking like a lush goddess standing before him in her beautiful black dinner dress, with tiny little black heels decorating her adorable feet and the golden glow from the fire roaring at her back. They'd talked of marriage since that first night, but he'd wanted to give her the seduction and romance that she deserved, and last night had definitely been that.

And after she'd given him her husky yes and a breathtaking smile, those beautiful brown eyes glistening with emotion, he'd lifted her dress and ripped off her minuscule lace panties. Then he'd treated himself to a taste of heaven right there between those soft thighs, eating her pretty, delicious little cunt until she'd come around his tongue and spilled those sweet pussy juices right down his throat.

Damn. His cock jumped to attention again at the vivid memory, and he silently groaned, forcing his attention back to the man standing in front of him.

"Congratulations," Jonah murmured, slapping his shoulder once more, before shoving his hands deep into his pockets. "It couldn't have happened to a better man. You're a lucky bastard, you know that?"

"I'll never forget it."

"I'll see that you don't," Jonah laughed, and Gabriel muttered, "Jackass," though he did it with his smile still firmly in place.

"You know, I really am happy for you," Jonah said, looking almost serious for a moment, his blue eyes dark and intense as he chuckled and added, "even though I was tempted to fight you for her, there for a while."

Gabriel cocked his head to the side as he studied him. "Yeah, I know you were. But, then, I also know that you understand she's mine," he replied with a hard grin.

Jonah nodded, and a dark, auburn lock of hair fell over his forehead, his blue eyes bright with mischief. "Yeah, I got that. That's why *I* let you have her."

"You mean it's why *I* let you live," Gabriel snorted, glad that they were able to joke about it, and that their friendship had survived, as strong as ever.

Grinning with his cocky arrogance, Jonah simply shrugged. "That's neither here nor there, since she's obviously yours."

"And if you were smart, you'd be out there finding your own."

Jonah nodded again, appearing lost in thought for a moment, before quickly shaking off whatever had snagged his attention. "Maybe you're right, man. Maybe you're right. And for what it's worth, if I know anyone who deserves some fucking happiness in their life, it's you, bro."

"And couldn't the same be said of you?"

"Jesus," Jonah snickered, "whatever you do, don't go letting Denny play matchmaker for me. She had me cornered in the break room today, trying to convince me I should ask out that little mouse who replaced her downstairs. I barely made it out in one piece."

He shook his head and laughed. "She wants to see you happy. And," Gabriel drawled, "we both think it's time you stopped living in your own screwed-up past, and quit comparing every woman you meet to that ruthless bitch who fucked you over."

Jonah shrugged defensively. "Hey, I didn't compare Denny to her."

Gabriel snorted again, knowing full well that Jonah was only trying to change the subject. "Leave my woman out of it, pal, and go find your own. Hell, maybe Denny's right about Jocelyn Brenna. I don't know why you're so damn hard on her. She's cute and sweet and—"

"Yeah," Jonah muttered, taking one hand out of his pocket to rub at the back of his neck, just like he always did when he was tense, "and she shoots daggers at me every time I fucking look at her. Drives me nuts. I don't know what Denny's thinking, but Jace Brenna just rubs me the wrong way."

Gabriel narrowed his eyes, suddenly wondering if Denny hadn't hit on something here with her amazing perception. Of course, he found everything about her amazing, he thought with a wry inner smile. "And maybe," he drawled, jerking his chin at the frowning redhead, "that's just because you're lying to yourself about how badly you'd like to be *rubbing* up against her."

"Oh hell," Jonah snickered, "I'm so outta here." His easy smile returned, blue eyes glittering with laughter. "And you should get your own ass outta here and go take care of your woman."

"That reminds me. You'll need to keep April free since you're the best man," he said as they moved apart.

"Wouldn't have it any other way," Jonah called back with a grin.

"Hey, and just think about what I said, man."

"God help me," Jonah muttered as he walked away, but Gabriel could hear his smiling laughter, and knew he wasn't angry. And he also suspected that the guy really *was* lying to himself. He was going to have to remember to ask Denny what she was planning for those two.

A few seconds later, he was standing outside his office door, and his gut went tight with anticipation, while he finally let loose on his control and allowed the blood to rush to his groin in a fierce, thick wave of arousal. His cock went painfully hard at the thought of Denny waiting for him inside, a heady combination of lust and love raging through his body that never failed to amaze him. And there was an even deeper, more primitive surge pumping through his blood at the thought of the four carat diamond sitting on her slim finger, proof of his claim on the woman who owned his heart and always would.

He turned the knob, and sure enough, there she was, perched on the edge of his desk, her feet propped on the seat of his leather chair with a bridal magazine laid across her cute knees, her feminine little fingers slowly flipping through the glossy pages. She looked over her shoulder at the sound of the door, and sent him a warm smile that shot straight down to the aching head of his dick, and he made sure to lock the door behind him as he stepped into the room.

"Hi there," she said, and the husky notes of her voice curled into him like a sweet, sun-warmed breeze, stroking his senses in a way that no other ever had…and no other ever would. He was an utterly taken man, and the woman who owned him sat right before him, looking good enough to eat.

Damn, but he loved her.

"Hi there yourself," he growled, suddenly wanting to beat his chest with pride like Tarzan at the sight of the sparkling rock on her finger, its exquisitely cut surface catching the brilliant rays of sunlight sneaking in through his slatted blinds.

"Are those for me?" she asked with an impish smile, setting aside the magazine as he walked toward her, those big brown eyes shining as she looked at the beautiful bouquet he held in his hand.

Gabriel smiled as she took the flowers and held them to her chest with a girlish squeal of delight. "Like you even had to ask."

"Thank you," she sighed, breathing in their rich perfume. "They're exquisite."

"Like you," he rumbled, sending the chair careening across the floor with a shove from his foot, then claiming its place before her. He set his briefcase on the floor, and then his warm palms found her soft thighs, urging them apart, his big hands taking the hem of her dress with them as they trailed higher and higher. He curved his fingers around her sweet bottom and pulled her to the edge of the desk as he stepped forward, bringing her flush against him.

"Exquisite, hmm?" she murmured, and that shy smile that he loved to distraction played over the rosy sheen of her petal-soft lips. "I'm afraid that flattery will get you anything," she laughed as he leaned down to nibble on the side of her throat, his hands taking the bouquet from her fingers, then setting the flowers gently on his desk. He pressed a tender kiss to the underside of her jaw and she moaned, bringing her legs up around his hips so that she cradled his heavy erection against the gentle cushion of her pussy.

"I don't need anything else, Denny." He kissed the corner of her eye, the gentle arc of her cheekbone. "I've got everything I could ever want right here."

"Me too," she moaned into his mouth as he went in for a hot, full, eating kiss that robbed them both of breath.

"Christ," he groaned, nibbling on her lower lip, swiping his tongue into the moist, sweet recess, loving the feel and taste of her, never able to get enough. "I missed you today."

She shot him a grinning look as she pulled back, shaking her head. "You were only gone for four hours!"

"Felt like four days," he growled, pressing his forehead to her own, wondering if he should just take her right there, on his desk, with a building full of people probably waiting to interrupt them, or if he should rush her ass home, to where he could give her his gift...and spend the rest of the night buried deep inside of her.

"Well, you'll be pleased to know that I spent the morning downstairs with Jace, while you were at your meeting, and I think she's going to be ready to be on her own soon."

"Thank God. I'm tired of you spending so much damn time down there."

"Yeah, and just where should I be spending my time?"

"In here," he growled, "with me. Or better yet, clamped around me, while I cram your sweet little cunt full with this big, hungry dick and fuck your beautiful little brains out."

"Mmm...sounds fun," she murmured, giggling as she reached around his waist and pinched his backside, making him laugh.

"And the second I have everything wrapped up here, you're going to be spending every second of every day with me, on those white sand beaches in the south of France."

After years of working without a break, he was finally taking some well-earned time off and spending it in a private villa on the Côte d'Azur, where he planned on doing nothing but gorging himself on his beautiful wife. Then, when they finally made it back home, he was going to start splitting his time between his home office and this one, instead of running himself into the ground, like he'd done for years.

And even though they were both desperate for children, they'd decided to give themselves a few years together, just the two of them at first. Of course, Denny had argued that until they did start a family, she could at least work part-time. Gabriel had disagreed, but he'd been unable to change the stubborn woman's mind, and so he'd hired Jocelyn Brenna part-time, to cover the hours that Denny wouldn't be there.

"Sunshine, sunsets, and a sexy stud," Denny purred, looking at him through her lashes. "What more could a girl want?"

"Whatever she wants, it's hers," he said in a low voice, meaning every word as he pulled her hands from around his waist and pressed her palms against the pounding of his heart.

She sighed dramatically and shook her head. "You're going to spoil me, Mr. Harrison."

"I plan on doing a hell of a lot more than that, Miss Abbott," he growled playfully, lifting her right hand to place a kiss beside his ring, "just as soon as I get your sweet little ass home. So let's get the hell out of here."

Denny tsked under her breath, sending him a mock look of reproach. "Are you forgetting that Lucas asked you to wait for him, so he can talk over the McCafferty account with you before we leave?"

"Damn," he muttered. "And here I thought I was only seconds away from stealing you outta here, getting you home, and taking you to bed. Where, I might add, I plan on keeping you 'til morning."

She pressed a tender kiss to his chin, then grinned up at him. "You're a devil, you know that?"

Gabriel gave her a long, heated look, and the wicked curve of his mouth, along with the glittering excitement in his eyes, made her gaze narrow in suspicion. "What?"

"Did I mention that I have a present for you tonight?"

"Oh yeah?" she said with her saucy smile, its giving heat so warm, he burned with it.

"Hmm…yeah, and you're going to look so beautiful wearing it," he rasped, his voice already going husky with desire and the heavy, aching throb of anticipation.

"You didn't buy me more clothes, did you?" she groaned, and he could see that she was ready to tease him again for his outrageous spending habits.

"Relax, angel," he laughed. "I swear it isn't more clothes. And no, it's not more shoes or jewelry either," he added, when she opened her mouth.

"Then how am I going to wear it?" she asked, sending him a wary look.

"Well, first I'm going to take you home tonight and fuck you silly. Then I'll probably have to fuck you silly again, since I'll be so turned on. By the third time, I'm hoping I'll be able to control myself long enough to lay you out on the bed and stuff your pretty new present up that beautiful, juicy pussy of yours that I love so much. And finally, when I've got you screaming, begging me in that sweet way of yours that makes my cock hard as nails, I'm going to pack this precious little ass full of *me*."

She groaned, shivering, then wet her mouth, and his eyes eagerly followed the sweeping action of her pink tongue across that plump, glossy lower lip that he wanted to devour. "Sounds full."

He sent her a hard, wolfish grin. "It will be."

"I can't believe you bought me a….er…"

"A dildo?" he teased, loving that she could still blush after everything he'd done to her…and planned on doing to her lush, gorgeous bod in the years to come.

"Sex toy," she sniffed, hiding behind the fall of her hair as her face turned crimson. "I was going to say 'sex toy,' you jerk. And stop teasing me."

"Okay, okay," he laughed as she swatted at his chest. He caught her hands and pressed them back against his chest. "Then, while we're waiting for Lucas and you're letting that evil little imagination of yours go wild about tonight, why don't you tell me about Jonah and Jocelyn Brenna?"

He had to give her points that she didn't even bat a lash.

"Don't give me that innocent look, you little imp," he rumbled. "I know you're up to something with those two."

Denny gave a dainty shrug of her shoulders, tucking a stray stand of mahogany hair behind the shell of her ear. "And would that be so bad?"

"Well, before you get your heart set on hooking those two up, I gotta warn you, angel. I'm not really certain that he likes her all that much."

"No," she said thoughtfully, "I don't think that's it. I think he's afraid of her."

"Of Miss Brenna?" he snorted. "She couldn't scare a mouse."

The delicate slopes of her brows pulled together in a reproving frown. "Stop it, Gabe. She isn't like that. She works like a demon and she's tough on the inside, even if she does look a little…"

"Angelic?" he offered helpfully.

"Yes," she muttered, breathing the word out on a sigh.

"Yeah, well, I doubt she's tough enough to handle a guy like Jonah, Denny. It's not every woman who'd be willing to put up with his…uh…"

"Fetishes? Scandalous proclivities? Baser needs?" she teased, eyes sparkling with humor when he seemed at a momentary loss for words.

"I'll show you baser needs," he said with another playful growl, nipping at her throat.

She tried to frown at him, but the effect was ruined by the laughter bubbling in her throat. "I'm serious, Gabriel. I think she may be just what he needs, instead of those snobby jerks he hangs out with at that club of his."

"I'll agree that he definitely needs a woman of his own," he smiled. "Someone who'll keep him on his toes, but he's going to have to catch her without my help. I'm taken."

"Yes," she agreed with a soft laugh, "you are most definitely taken, gorgeous. And would you say I keep you on your toes?"

"Ah angel, you've got me any way you want me. On my toes, my knees, wrapped around your little finger. I'm a slave," he rasped, rubbing the gritty words into her moist, succulent lips, then following with a long, stroking lick of his hungry tongue. God, she tasted so good, he wanted to lap her up, like a cat with cream. Wanted to consume her, one delicious piece at a time. "And I'm done talking about Jonah."

She arched against him, moaning into his mouth, arms thrown around his neck, holding tight, and he felt that flash of need ignite in her body. Felt the shift from simmering want to raging, primitive hunger as if it were his own.

"My wicked little Denny. You need to be fucked again, right now, don't you, angel?" he rasped, gripping her hips to pull her closer...tighter...trapping her against the aching ridge of his pants-covered cock.

"Lucas isn't going to be here for another twenty minutes," she gasped, breathing the husky words into his mouth as she nipped at his bottom lip, rubbing the moist crotch of her panties against his distended fly, and he felt the rumbling growl that broke from his throat all the way down in the soles of his feet. "And you know what they say, devil man," she purred. "No rest for the wicked."

He lifted his face, capturing her brilliant, love-filled gaze, and groaned with savage satisfaction at what he saw shining there.

"Come on," she drawled, lowering her lashes as she sent him a teasing, challenging look that damn near made his blood boil. "Let's see how quickly you can make me scream. I dare ya," she added in a throaty whisper, pulling that lush lower lip through her teeth.

A harsh, happy laugh broke out of his chest, a brilliant wave of heat, like melted sunshine, warming his soul...and then Gabriel showed *his woman* just how wicked he could be.

Why an electronic book?

We live in the Information Age—an exciting time in the history of human civilization, in which technology rules supreme and continues to progress in leaps and bounds every minute of every day. For a multitude of reasons, more and more avid literary fans are opting to purchase e-books instead of paper books. The question from those not yet initiated into the world of electronic reading is simply: *Why?*

1. *Price.* An electronic title at Ellora's Cave Publishing and Cerridwen Press runs anywhere from 40% to 75% less than the cover price of the exact same title in paperback format. Why? Basic mathematics and cost. It is less expensive to publish an e-book (no paper and printing, no warehousing and shipping) than it is to publish a paperback, so the savings are passed along to the consumer.

2. *Space.* Running out of room in your house for your books? That is one worry you will never have with electronic books. For a low one-time cost, you can purchase a handheld device specifically designed for e-reading. Many e-readers have large, convenient screens for viewing. Better yet, hundreds of titles can be stored within your new library—on a single microchip. There are a variety of e-readers from different manufacturers. You can also read e-books on your PC or laptop computer. (Please note that Ellora's Cave does not endorse any specific brands.

You can check our websites at www.ellorascave.com or www.cerridwenpress.com for information we make available to new consumers.)

3. *Mobility.* Because your new e-library consists of only a microchip within a small, easily transportable e-reader, your entire cache of books can be taken with you wherever you go.

4. *Personal Viewing Preferences.* Are the words you are currently reading too small? Too large? Too... ANNOYING? Paperback books cannot be modified according to personal preferences, but e-books can.

5. *Instant Gratification.* Is it the middle of the night and all the bookstores near you are closed? Are you tired of waiting days, sometimes weeks, for bookstores to ship the novels you bought? Ellora's Cave Publishing sells instantaneous downloads twenty-four hours a day, seven days a week, every day of the year. Our webstore is never closed. Our e-book delivery system is 100% automated, meaning your order is filled as soon as you pay for it.

Those are a few of the top reasons why electronic books are replacing paperbacks for many avid readers.

As always, Ellora's Cave and Cerridwen Press welcome your questions and comments. We invite you to email us at Comments@ellorascave.com or write to us directly at Ellora's Cave Publishing Inc., 1056 Home Avenue, Akron, OH 44310-3502.

Cerridwen, the Celtic Goddess of wisdom, was the muse who brought inspiration to storytellers and those in the creative arts. Cerridwen Press encompasses the best and most innovative stories in all genres of today's fiction. Visit our site and discover the newest titles by talented authors who still get inspired - much like the ancient storytellers did, once upon a time.

Cerridwen Press

www.cerridwenpress.com

*Discover for yourself why readers can't get enough
of the multiple award-winning publisher*

Ellora's Cave.

Whether you prefer e-books or paperbacks,

*be sure to visit EC on the web at
www.ellorascave.com*

*for an erotic reading experience that will leave you
breathless.*